LOVE AND PIRATES

RUSS HALL

AUTHOR OF THE AL QUINN SERIES

---

1.   http://StreetlightGraphics.com

Chapter 1

He came down the dim stairs more slowly than usual and stepped out onto the sidewalk. The bright glare of the sun blinded him for a moment. He blinked and could see her standing across the street. She was trying unsuccessfully to act like she wasn't waiting on him. Ivy Palmer, pale blond hair and athletically slim. Her smile was like the sun coming out from behind clouds.

Everything about her should have attracted him to her.

She looked like she was about to cross the street to where he stood. A string of three cars passed in front of where she planned to jaywalk.

He spun and started up the sidewalk as briskly as he could go without seeming to jog away.

"Hardy! Hardy Hanlon!" she yelled across the street. "Wait up."

He wanted to break into a run. Instead, he stopped until she could sprint across the street at her first opportunity. She made it halfway across in one rush, waited until two more cars went past and the two lanes going the other direction were clear, then ran across. As soon as she was beside him, he started walking again. He held his gym bag in his right hand, on the other side from her. He switched it to his left hand so he could ease around and walk on the outside of the sidewalk.

"I'll bet one of your parents told you that was the gallant thing to do," she said.

The subject had never come up, so she couldn't know his parents had died when he was young. He'd grown up in an orphanage—well, sort of one. He had never been taken home by foster parents. But he had read in books that walking on the outside not only protected the female but, in the early days of chivalry, protected the female from people throwing slops and emptying chamber pots from second-story windows, the contents usually landing to the outside of walkways rather than the inside.

She glanced at him when he didn't respond. She had tried to be friendlier to him several times, but he hadn't encouraged it.

Baytown kept up its usual midday bustle around them. Horns tooted. Buses rumbled past on their routes. Waves of heat came up from the pavement as they passed.

"Where are you headed?" she asked.

"Down toward the water."

"I'm sorry you can't work on Dad's boat anymore."

He shrugged. "I was glad for the work. It helped me pay my way through school. That's done now. So I was going to have to figure something else out anyway."

"You still have your job at the gym, don't you?"

"Today was the last day for that."

"Oh." She paused. "I guess I did hear the old place was closing. The whole block is going to be knocked down, right? Some sort of mall for boutique shops."

He looked up. The sky was a cloudless blue with a steady breeze from the ocean sweeping across the city and Connecticut. Grey storm clouds would have better suited his mood.

He could see the basketball court ahead. Three juniors from his college were playing half-court basketball. He thought about crossing to the other side of the street, but they'd already seen him.

"There he is. Old Windy Hanlon. Why don't you get up and say a few words?" Whit stood with the basketball on one hip. He played varsity football as well as basketball. He'd been recruited from somewhere out where wheat and corn grew—Nebraska or Kansas, something like that. He had grown tall out there.

"Just ignore them," Hardy said to Ivy, keeping his voice low.

"Hey, Hardy, I heard you once broke an air guitar," J.J., the smallest of them, said. His dark face twisted into a grin that was half sneer. He was the fastest player on the team and ran track as well.

Hardy kept moving. They were halfway past the court, with a chain-link fence between him and the players.

"Naw, that was no air guitar," Braxton said. "Word has it he sexually harassed himself all through high school." He had the broad shoulders of a power forward. He came from upstate New York and had worn his blond hair long, like a Viking, until the coach ordered him to get a buzz cut. He had switched to pulling his hair back into a ponytail instead, ignoring the coach, who needed him on the team enough not to push too hard.

"Why are they so angry with you?" Ivy whispered.

"I heard that his income, like his love life, is mostly imaginary." Whit smirked.

"Hardy har har," Braxton said.

Hardy leaned closer to whisper into the delicate shell of Ivy's ear. "All the students at the college were made to attend the graduation ceremony."

"And that made them mad?" she whispered back.

"I was valedictorian. I had to give a speech. I didn't want to, but they said I had to do it. So I kept it short."

"But long enough to fire up these guys, it seems," she said.

Hardy shook his head. "Shouldn't have. They're hard to figure."

"Probably envy," she muttered. To the players, she yelled, "Leave him alone!"

"Oh, that'll help." Hardy started walking faster.

"You don't have to fight his battles for him, Miss High-and-Mighty Palmer!" Whit yelled.

J.J. moved closer to the fence. "I bet she told you she was on the pill. But she didn't tell you that the pill was penicillin."

"What is wrong with you boys?" Ivy said. "Insufferable jerks."

The players broke into a run, leaving the basketball behind to roll out of bounds. They got to the end of the fence and stepped out onto the sidewalk to stand in front of Hardy and Ivy.

Hardy glanced at the traffic, which was too steady to consider a quick dash to the other side of the street. Besides, that would just entice this lot. They were already stirred to a near boil.

"Where do you think you're going in such a hurry?" Braxton asked.

Hardy didn't answer. He took his time sizing them up, guessing who would make the first move.

J.J. in particular was breathing harder, like a little banty rooster, though he was slightly bigger than Hardy. "You know, we're not idiots. We don't think innuendo is an Italian suppository."

"Well, you are certainly trying over hard to be clever," Ivy said. "Are you compensating?"

You're not helping here, Ivy, Hardy thought.

Whit stepped forward toward her.

Hardy slipped between them so Whit towered over Hardy. Whit put a hand big enough to palm a basketball on Hardy's chest and pushed him aside.

Hardy straightened himself and slipped back between them, looking up at Whit. "Please don't do that."

"Do what?" Whit put his hand on Hardy's chest again.

But as he pushed hard this time, Hardy dropped his gym bag, pressed both of his hands on the back of Whit's and, bending forward, snapped rapidly to his right, his elbow catching Whit's forearm and sweeping it along. He put his whole body's weight and strength into the move.

"What the...?" Before Whit could finish, big as he was, he spun in the air and went into a sideways roll that took him to the chain-link fence.

J.J. rushed forward with his hands extended to grab Hardy, who grabbed the arms, turned his back to J.J., and sent him flying in the air to land in a hard flop on his back.

Braxton flexed his chest and arms. He ran at Hardy like a bull. Hardy swept the hands away and stepped in to grab Braxton's lowered head from above. Braxton's weight and the momentum of his run took him to his knees while Hardy cut off all the air going to that oversized head.

Braxton's hands swept up to punch at Hardy, but they began to weaken and then lowered. Hardy let go, and Braxton slumped to the sidewalk, gasping for air.

Whit and J.J. had been slow getting to their feet. They looked down at Braxton, and neither seemed inclined to have another go at Hardy. Braxton was on his knees, gasping for breath, but eager to go again.

Whit put a hand down and held him in place. "Let it go. Even if we knock his eyebrows off, one of us might get injured, and that would mean sitting on the bench for a season."

"Come on," Hardy said to Ivy. He picked up his gym bag and started off in the direction they had been headed.

Ivy glanced back a couple of times as they got to the end of the block and crossed the street. "They're staying back there."

"Good."

"I wouldn't have believed that if I hadn't seen it."

"They probably feel the same way."

"I heard you taught some sort of class at the gym. Was it about that stuff?"

"I was a wrestler in high school. When I tried out for that team in college, the other guys in my weight class were way too experienced and sophisticated for me. So I started taking judo at the gym. I moved on from that to jiu-jitsu and worked at it long enough to teach a few courses on self-defense and such."

He didn't mention that the reason he had been a wrestler in high school was because it was sort of a solo sport, just one person against another on the mat. That's the way he had worked best, alone. He had been undefeated at that level because he had an absolute fear of losing. A much bigger wrestler in practice had once had him down, pressing his face hard against the spongy rubber mat. From somewhere deep inside, Hardy had summoned a burst of drive and strength. He had wrenched away at one of the gripping arms, twisting it as he stood, to lift the bigger guy up onto his toes. In a moment, Hardy had reversed the situation and had his opponent in a pin position. He'd had to stretch his toes out as far as they could go and hold tight while waiting for the guy's neck bridge to tire. Finally, the guy had flopped to the mat, and Hardy had pinned him.

Chapter 2

"Where are we going?" Ivy asked.

"We?" Hardy wanted to ask her why she was still tagging along but feared the candid answer he might get. "I wanted to have a look at the ocean."

They were close enough already to smell the salt in the air and hear the *kree, kree* of the gulls, soaring and dipping in the shoreline thermals.

They walked in silence until they came to a row of piers and docks. Hardy could look out at the boats bobbing at their moorings in the harbor, but he couldn't see *Pequod II*, Mr. Palmer's fifty-foot yacht. Nor could he expect to find the Palmer's Zodiac RIB stored where it was usually kept to be used as a dinghy to get out to the yacht's mooring.

A row of benches ran along the sidewalk that went past the docks. Hardy plopped onto one, took a deep breath of salty air, and looked out across the water. He could feel the breeze rub his cheeks and could see whitecaps on the crests of waves in the distance. The wind was vigorous enough for some hearty sailing.

"Is that what you want?" she asked as she sat down beside him but on the other side of his gym bag.

"What?" He turned to her.

She had the face of a chipmunk up to something when she suppressed her grin the way she was doing, not altogether successfully. She wasn't what some people would call pretty, but her folks had money, and she was always well-dressed and made over to emphasize her strengths. When relaxed, she could look like a nerdy farm girl, a combination Hardy found particularly attractive and appealing. But rich.

That slowed his thoughts in that direction. He looked back out to the ocean. A tanker was sliding slowly across the horizon. Most of the fishing boats were either still far out of sight or docked after an early start and their crews resting before another morning of heading out to sea.

"You'd like to be out there, wouldn't you?" she said.

"Out where?"

"On the ocean. Sailing away."

He turned to her. She was grinning outright now.

But she had been spot on. That was what he did want more than anything. He could envision himself as a crew member of a clipper ship or a brig like the *Pilgrim*. He would scramble up into the rigging to furl the sails or to let out the sheets when they were to run full out with the wind.

He had gone down into the hull of the *USS Constitution* once on a trip to Boston. Feeling "Old Ironsides" around him as he bobbed in the water had tickled his lust to be a crewmember at sea. Maybe he'd been born too late. But people still worked on the ocean—maybe not always on sailing ships, but there were still some salty jobs out there.

"I've thought about it a time or two," he admitted.

"You usually seem a happy, cheerful person. But you seem a little pensive and withdrawn today."

He shrugged.

They both stared out for a while at the distant waves.

"What was wrong with those guys back there?" She finally broke her silence.

He started to shrug again, stopped himself, but said nothing.

"That was not normal behavior at all," she said.

"It's something I've been trying to figure out," he said. "It's a national mood thing. Lately, people seem hair-triggered and ready to tee off against anything that even mildly irks them."

"And these guys?"

"They're probably feeling chapped in general because they play their sports at a place like Cooper College instead of a top-ten Division One school."

"Whatever did you say in that ever-so-brief valedictorian speech that rubbed them the wrong way?"

"Very darn little. I just said to my assembled classmates, 'I'm as surprised about this as you are. Stay curious. Be kind.' That was the whole speech, and I sat down."

"Telling them to be kind made them hostile?" She shook her head. "I'm hard pressed to understand how encouraging people to be kind made them mad enough to want to beat you up. Do you think it was the brevity of your speech that annoyed them?"

"They've been bumping into me in the hallways for most of the semester."

"Ever since you were named class valedictorian, right? Bunch of jocks."

"Hey, I'm kind of a jock, of a different sort. They were itching and spoiling to be mad about something. I was convenient."

"Whatever it was, they seem the bully sort, and you were somehow kicking sand in their faces. Maybe their awareness that you were getting good grades made you suddenly into a nerd, their sworn enemy."

"Life doesn't have to be about opposites. The Hatfield-McCoy feud days are long gone."

"No, they're not," she said. "It's one political party against the other, one religion against another, one race against another, and this school's team against another school's team. People are grabbing at opportunities to unite in one bunch just to hate another bunch. It's nonsensical, and it's maddening. But it's happening. People seem to be getting stewed in the brine that leads to divisiveness... and conflict. You're a firsthand witness to that."

He looked out across the water, which stretched as far as he could see. "It's a wide and complex world these days, and I've only seen a sliver or two of it yet. Maybe when I've seen more, I'll understand what's generating a mood that encourages and tolerates that sort of thing."

"I guess I just don't understand senseless hate. Even animals in the wild don't have that. And all you did was ask them to be kind."

"These are the sort of guys who get ticked off if you tell them to have a nice day. They don't like anyone telling them to do anything. That may be just one of the reasons they aren't at a Division One school."

"Do you have regrets about not attending one of the big-name schools yourself?"

"You're going to Yale, right?"

She nodded.

"And you didn't get in by being a nonparticipating member of the rowing team or a nonplaying member of the tennis team, did you?"

"Of course not. You should know a thing or two about getting good grades. It's just hard work, late nights, and a hunger that drives you."

He had used the word "curiosity," but he could have said "intellectual lust" as well, a need to see, explore, and to know more.

She lowered his gym bag to the ground and tried to slide closer.

He stood up. "Look, I've got to go. I need to find a place to stay tonight."

"Oh, that's right. You were living in a back room at the gym, weren't you? But it's..."

"Closing. Right." He bent and picked up his gym bag, which held everything he owned: a spare shirt, clean underwear, his gym clothes, which he'd taken the time to wash, his shaving and toothbrushing kit, and one book.

"I don't know how much more obvious I can get, but I'd like to get to know you better." She looked up at him with that perky face that could also seem sad.

"We're worlds apart."

"We don't have to be." Her pale-blue eyes managed to look pleading and eager at the same time.

Her father, Reginald Palmer, whom no one dared call Reggie, was old-money rich, the kind of man foolish and sentimental enough to send his yacht across America instead of just getting a new one on the west coast. He wouldn't fancy someone dating his daughter who happened to be the guy who scrubbed his boat until it was sparkling clean in Bristol fashion and was ready to go out to sea each time Palmer wanted to sail. Hardy knew he had something like forty-seven dollars in his wallet. Mr. Palmer probably had that many millions or perhaps way more. Hardy couldn't get his head around that kind of money. He wasn't even sure how Ivy could be interested in a bit of driftwood like himself. She'd met him only a few times, and he'd often been scruffy and dirty from tending to the boat.

"Look, I've got to get going." He spun and started off. He didn't look back.

As he walked, he could smell a pizza shop across the street. A block later, he caught a whiff of Chinese food. His stomach gave an eager lurch, but he needed to be careful about how much money he spent just now.

The sun was nestling into the trees on the western horizon by the time he got to where the boat was waiting for its trip. The sky was beginning to dim the way it does along the eastern coastline as dusk came quickly with the dark of night hard on its heels.

The *Pequod II* sat up on the bed of a yacht-transport truck, all ready to take off toward its new home come dawn. The driver had deadheaded all the way from California and was catching up on his sleep before heading back. The semi rig had a sleeping compartment behind the cab, but the driver would get plenty enough of that before the yacht was slipped into the waters of the Pacific Ocean.

Hardy felt in his pocket. He still had the key, the only key he had left since the gym and his sad little apartment in the back end of the gym had been locked shut for the last time. He glanced around. He had to sleep somewhere.

He clambered up the back of the truck and then got up the stern ladder until he stood on the deck. The masts had been lowered and lay across the middle of the yacht. The Zodiac that Palmer used to get to the boat's mooring from shore was held tightly in place on the deck with sturdy bungee cords. He was sure going to miss this old tub even though he had polished its brass until his fingers ached and scrubbed its teak deck with a holystone until he could barely stand up straight. Maybe it was a love-hate thing.

He glanced around. No one appeared to be around. He went over to where the hatch was locked. He took out his key, opened the hatch, and pulled it closed again as he went below. Little light came in since most of the portholes were closed. But he knew his way across to the fridge he had emptied just a day before. He opened the door, and the light didn't come on. All of the boat's power was off.

It was a wooden Arabesque-style yacht without a lot of the bells and whistles of the more modern plastic-looking boats. Yet it was well maintained and restored where it needed to be. It had the minimal conveniences, power from a 5.5-kilowatt genset generator, and water for the tiny galley and head. The rest was almost like sailing in the old days.

Her sail handling could be done by a push button from the helm with a hydraulically controlled main sheet, two-speed electric winches, hydraulic roller furling, hydraulic backstay and outer forestay, and electric boom furling. One person could sail her.

And sail? Reginald Palmer himself claimed the boat was the Ferrari of sailing boats.

She had a cold-molded wooden hull, a teak-over-plywood deck, and wooden cabin and cockpit structures. The rig was carbon fiber with in-boom furling and twin roller-furling head stays including a large genoa for light air conditions. With a fin keel and bow thruster, she could be easily handled when in a harbor. Below, the cabin was finished with South American mahogany and polished brass instead of the standard stainless steel.

Reginald Palmer was a minimalist, which Hardy liked. He'd kept the cabin bare, just the bed, galley, and head. No cushioned seating ran along its sides, except for in the small breakfast nook with table fixed in place. The rest of the cabin floor was bare teak, which Hardy also got to scrub regularly.

Hardy felt his way to the bed he'd made. The covers were tight enough to bounce a quarter into the air off them. But he stretched out anyway. He could make it again before he left. Just a few minutes—all he needed was a few minutes.

He reached for the hand light in its holder beside the bed. When he flipped the switch, he got a good, solid beam. It still had some juice in it, though it couldn't recharge until the boat had power again.

From his gym bag he took out his worn leather-bound copy of Dana's *Two Years before the Mast.* He had read the book so many times the binding was soft to his touch and the bookmark ribbon was fraying at the end. Hardy flipped through the pages until he got to the section where Dana was going around the Horn, clinging to frozen rigging as he pounded at the cloth of a sail with his fist as he fought to furl it against the relentless force of the wind.

He thought his eyes had only flickered shut for a moment or two. The sound of the truck starting awakened him. His eyes snapped open. More light was coming through the portholes, the light of early dawn. The yacht gave a lurch as the truck shifted into gear. Hardy went over to one of the open portholes and looked out. They were rolling. The yacht was off on its way across America, and he was in it.

Chapter 3

Hardy hadn't been too surprised when he'd learned that Connecticut's state insect was the praying mantis, in which the mating male often loses his head and is eaten, a story with a moral even Aesop may have overlooked. It seemed apt enough to him since that pretty much summed up how his few relations with the fairer sex seemed to have gone.

"Oh my gosh." Hardy jumped up from the bed and looked out the nearest porthole. The buildings of Baytown were zipping past.

His heart pumped fast, and his stomach felt like it wanted to crawl up through his throat.

He rushed to the hatch, opened it, and scrambled out onto the deck. Anywhere he might try to stand on the deck and wave to the driver was obscured by the bulk of the yacht.

An emergency flare gun was in the kit on the Zodiac, and another was at the helm. He could hardly fire either of those into the street ahead.

He racked his brain for a way to reach the driver and stop him. If he'd had a phone, it wouldn't have helped him since he didn't know the driver's number. The boat's ship-to-shore radio was shut down like everything else electronic in the boat.

As they rolled past the stores and businesses, approaching the outskirts of Baytown, he realized people on the sidewalks and inside the restaurants and stores might see him. Maybe even people in the cars and trucks of the traffic could see him. For a second, he wondered if he could wave to any of them to try to stop the truck.

He paused for just a moment to think about that.

Instead of waving to them for help to stop the driver, he dropped to the deck. He had no reason to stay in Baytown. His jobs were at an end, as were his college days. There was no one in the area who cared about him, except possibly that Palmer girl.

He looked up at the sky as the yacht went by beneath it. When he sat up, the wind swept across his face and tugged at his short hair. It felt a lot like being at sea except he could see houses, buildings, and patches of green trees rolling past. He stretched back out on the deck and watched the smattering of clouds and blue sky.

The next time he peeked over the gunwale at the last of the town going by, he began to enjoy the ride, the idea of going someplace. But he was a little conspicuous up on the deck, so he went back below, closing and locking the hatch behind himself.

Too many hours spent cleaning the inside of the yacht compelled him to make sure everything was shipshape. He put his book back in his gym bag and stowed that in a cabinet. He checked the hand light. He had fortunately turned it off before falling asleep. It still had a steady, firm beam, which he might need, and it couldn't recharge until the power was back on in the boat. He put it back in its holder beside the bed. Only when he had made the bed a taut surface again did he go over to look out the porthole.

The driver seemed to favor a leisurely pace. Even as the truck eased up a ramp onto the highway, he stayed in the right lane, barely keeping up with the speed limit. They rolled through a part of Connecticut Hardy hadn't seen often enough to know it well. The green hills and clusters of houses looked cozy and cheerful.

Maybe he was bringing some of that to the view. Not so very long ago, he had ridden on a train enough to savor looking out the windows. He had thought at the time that it would be nice to sit in one, watching America go by the window outside. Now, he was getting a taste of that and quite enjoying it.

He watched for several more miles before a hollow spot in his stomach reminded him he hadn't eaten. In the ship's galley, he looked around again though he knew Reginald Palmer had asked him to remove the supplies from the pantry and the extra dead weight of bottles of water. The plan was to buy all-new supplies on the west coast.

The fridge was empty and well cleaned. It was also off, with no power turned on in the boat. He was going to need food and water, especially water. In the back of the lowest pantry shelf, he found the one box he'd been told to leave in the yacht. It held a case of champagne, a brand Palmer favored. He could hardly drink that, though if he got thirstier than he was, it might come to that.

He went back to sitting by the porthole and looking outside, first on one side and then the other as the panorama of scenery constantly shifted and changed.

As long as he had lived in Connecticut, he had never seen or savored much of what was passing by him now. Out past the urban sprawl, he began to see small villages, farms with silos, piled stone fences, and a wooden covered bridge. A man in waders was fly-fishing in the stream. Green trees climbed a hill until stopped by a fence made of stone. Children played in the yard of a school.

He would see stretches of green, green, green in varied hues, in vertical and horizontal stripes. Then he'd get a burst of kaleidoscopic color—a red barn, a surprisingly yellow tractor, black-and-white cows. The sky would be bluer and the grass greener. Then the colors would swirl, merge, and melt into the metal, bricks, and glass of a passing city in the distance or a cluster of fast-food restaurants and gas stations flashing their eager, bright signs and lights down below a turnoff ramp.

This was the slice of America he had hoped to glimpse out a train window. Oh, frabjous joy! This was somewhere else, and he was whirling his way along through the heart of it all.

At the pace the truck was traveling, with many vehicles zipping by to its left, the drive to the New York state border took nearly two hours. Then Hardy watched the southern tip of New York roll by, with glimpses of large cities and climbing hills by the time they crossed the Hudson River.

He stayed glued to one porthole or another, trying hard not to think about his stomach.

At last, they crossed over into Pennsylvania, and the view was green, green, green. On the many hills, the truck had to labor when going up them and then coast on the down sides.

He had overheard Reginald say once that he would have liked for his yacht to travel eventually westward on Route 66. But he knew that route wasn't what it used to be, and it had never been best suited for hauling a large boat.

After a short while, the view out the starboard porthole settled into a monotonous stream of green hills with occasional side pockets of gas stations, truck stops, and fast-food restaurants. He began to wish Reginald had gotten his way. Route 66 or any of the more back roads might have offered more local color than an interstate route. But even with its masts down, a boat this size might have issues crowding its way along two-lane routes and weaving through the traffic of smaller towns.

On the one hand, it felt good to be moving along. But he did wish they could be taking the rural back roads where he could see Pennsylvania Dutch hex signs on barns, cattle grazing in richly green fields, and covered bridges over rippling streams. He had to agree that such a route would never do for hauling a yacht, though.

He went over to the other side and began to focus on the vehicles steadily passing them on that side. Quite a few of the passengers held cell phones and were looking into them with their whole fixed attention while the green world of nature rolled by. Whether they were talking to someone or surfing through the internet on the wheels of some search engine or other, their world seemed reduced to a small rectangular screen.

Crossing the state of Pennsylvania seemed to go on and on. He was beginning to wonder if the driver would ever stop to take a break, maybe at a truck stop where he could dash out and get water and food.

Most of the traffic Hardy could see going past out a porthole just zoomed by. One vehicle took its time. A purple Lincoln convertible eased up beside the truck. The driver wore a wide Panama hat that shaded his already dark face. The buxom white woman in the passenger seat wore a skimpy outfit of tank top over shorts with sandals. Large holes had been cut in the shorts and top so that significant parts of her poked out for easy viewing. The woman waved to the driver of the yacht's transport truck and gave a promising look as they went past.

A pimpmobile, Hardy thought to himself. *They're sure working this stretch of highway back and forth.*

When the truck's driver pulled into the next rest stop they came to, Hardy gave a sigh of relief. He watched out the window as the driver went across to the bathrooms. He waited until the driver had gone inside before he grabbed his toothpaste and toothbrush to sprint across the lot to the men's room.

As he neared it, he spotted the woman who had been the passenger in the purple Lincoln. The black driver—her pimp, no doubt—leaned against the side of their parked car. She was busy talking to a couple of men who had just come out of the bathroom.

He ducked around them and went inside. Hardy couldn't see the driver of his truck anywhere, though at least one of the toilet stall doors was closed. He had only moments.

Hardy made as quick a pit stop as he could, taking care of his bathroom needs, splashing water on his face, running his fingers through his short hair for a comb, and even giving his teeth a quick brush. In the mirror, putting aside the bemused look, he could see a shadow of stubble on his cheeks and chin. But he didn't dare take time for a quick shave, not that it mattered. He hurried out the door before the truck driver left his stall.

He looked around for anything like a vending machine, thinking dreamy thoughts of a Snickers bar or those cheese crackers with peanut butter fillings—something hearty. But he saw nothing, not even a soda machine. So he started for the truck before the driver could come out and see him, not that it mattered, when he thought about it, since the driver didn't know about his stowaway.

The hooker from the purple pimpmobile spotted him. She stepped in front of him as he sought to hurry back to the yacht. "Do you want to party?" she asked.

"Will there be cake?" he asked.

Her eyes opened wide at him. He used her confusion to step around her and break into a jog, getting back to the boat on its trailer.

He got back inside the yacht and closed and locked the hatch. Just a few moments later, he heard someone climb the ladder and move about on the deck, tug at the battened hatch, and then get back off the boat. That would have been the driver making sure nothing was shifting around.

As the truck jostled its way up the ramp, getting back on the interstate, a few things rattled around in a couple of cabinets and drawers. He went around and made sure everything was in its place, padded when possible, and as shipshape as it could be.

When he had prepped the ship for its passage across the continent, he'd tried to ensure that every little thing would travel well. Maybe it was a good thing he was along to make sure it all stayed that way.

The miles stretched on, and the cabin grew stuffy, but he didn't want to crack the hatch to let air inside. After a while, he got back onto the bed and did a little math in his head. The trip from coast to coast would probably be somewhere around three thousand miles. He doubted the driver would try to cover more than three hundred miles a day. Regular eighteen-wheel semi rig drivers probably shot for way more than that, grabbing naps in their sleeper compartments. But this driver seemed inclined to take a more leisurely pace.

Chapter 4

The next thing Hardy knew, he was waking from his nap to the sounds of the truck pulling off the highway. The close air in the cabin had been soporific. But he was glad he hadn't cracked the hatch for a flow of air. He heard the driver climb up just far enough to have a look around the deck once they were parked.

Hardy stayed away from the portholes until he heard the driver climb down the ladder. In a moment, he could see him walking away toward the restaurant front of a truck stop. The sky was fading quickly into the growing dark of dusk.

With no idea of how long it would take the driver to dine and return, he looked at himself in the mirror in the fading light of the head, which he could not use as a bathroom. The water reserve for that had been emptied.

He slipped outside the hatch, locked it behind himself, and crept to the gunwale and looked over. He could only see a driver here and there of any of the semi rigs parked in rows. Most were probably inside eating or perhaps in their sleeping compartments, resting before a renewed run at night. These were full-time truck drivers on tight schedules, unlike Hardy's driver, who he'd seen ambling as he headed toward the lights of the restaurant.

As soon as Hardy could see no movement, he climbed down the yacht's back ladder and clambered off the truck. Once on the asphalt parking lot, he tried not to look furtive. He borrowed the truck driver's saunter as he headed past the rows of gas and diesel pumps toward the convenience store side of the truck stop. He wanted to look like just another truck driver making a pit stop, but he suspected he looked nothing like most of the other truck drivers.

Although the sky was dark, the inside of the convenience store was lit up like a neon fart, a bright-white one.

Everything that could be white was white—the shelves, the walls, and even the checkout counter centered near the door.

The inside of the store was wide and open, extending all the way to the restaurant, where diners sat at the tables or the counter. His own driver sat with his back to the window so that he could look Hardy's way if he chose.

He made a quick visit to the huge men's room and saw a tempting sign that pointed to free showers in the next room. There was no time for shaving and showering. The driver could head back to the truck at any time. He went back out into the store.

Hardy kept his back to the restaurant side as much as he could while he quickly browsed for what he needed. A row of coffee urns emitted a faint smell of burned oil, the usual sign of not being cleaned often enough. A rotisserie of hot dogs went round and round. At least half the hot dogs had been on it long enough to wrinkle, so they looked like fingerprints. He also ignored a soup station with a couple of open containers of heated soups, doubting he could trust them.

There were rows upon rows of corn and potato chips, as well as sodas and beer. But he couldn't see any produce—no salads and not even apples. The restaurant probably had to do for any fresher foods like that, and he couldn't go there.

He scooped up a twelve-pack of bottled water, his chief need. The inside of his mouth was starting to feel like cotton. Next, he located a display of packets of beef, turkey, and bison jerky. But the prices were three times what he was used to at the grocery. He finally picked out a small eight-dollar pack of beef jerky he would have to make do. He needed protein, but he also needed to make his money last.

He looked up and saw another customer peering around an end-cap display of ball caps and fuzzy dice. Hardy had never seen fuzzy dice for sale anywhere before, and he'd always wondered where folks got the ones they hung in their cars and trucks. Now he knew.

The guy was still staring, practically leering now that Hardy was paying attention. He wondered if he knew this person from somewhere. It wasn't his driver.

The guy stepped out from behind the counter. He wore a checkered flannel shirt with the sleeves cut off, in a size big enough to cover a large pot belly that extended out over the top of his jeans.

He winked.

In a flash, Hardy understood. This lonely truck driver was making a pass, and not a very subtle one.

Hardy hurried to the checkout counter, scooping up a small flashlight and batteries. He had to read. But paying for his small purchases made a significant dent in his wallet.

The man was still staring at Hardy and winked again, more broadly this time. Hardy didn't share anything that might look like an encouraging smile. He clutched his plastic bag and twelve-pack of water and shot out the door.

He passed a You Are Here! sign outside the door that showed they were in the middle of Pennsylvania, still to the east of State College, which was in the dead center of the state. Years ago, when the state had gotten a university land grant, someone had drawn an X from corner to corner on the state and had decided to locate the school there.

Out at the back of the trailered yacht, he looked around before he climbed back up with his purchases. Once inside again, he locked the hatch behind himself. He allowed himself a few pieces of the jerky, opened one of the bottles of water, and sipped at it. He stowed the rest of the water and the jerky package in the small fridge, where there were straps to hold things in place while on the boat when it was out on the tossing sea.

Before he went to bed, he went around and looked out the open portholes but saw nothing other than here and there a strolling trucker. He'd made sure the lonely and overfriendly one inside hadn't followed him. Then he took his new flashlight and got on the bed, opening his copy of *Dana* to the flogging scene. He wasn't in the mood for that, so he flipped ahead to loading cattle hides on the California coast.

The moment he began to feel drowsy, he turned off the flashlight.

Perhaps three or four hours later, he woke.

Except for the distant sound of the highway and trucks using their air brakes as they slowed to pull into the truck stop, the night seemed still. The driver must have been asleep in the cab, he figured. The lights were still bright at the building though the sky looked black.

Hardy got out his shaving kit and went out through the hatch, locking it behind himself. Cloud cover obscured any sign of stars or the moon. The evening breeze felt cool as it swept over him. He climbed down and looked around.

An empty container of no-fat cottage cheese with a plastic spoon inside rested on the ground. It hardly seemed the sort of food he'd seen most of the truckers enjoying. He didn't see anyone moving about near him, so he headed for the building in hopes of a shower and a shave.

Only one or two truckers were being served in the restaurant. The convenience store was empty. Its checkout clerk was reading a newspaper spread across the counter. He didn't look up as Hardy crossed the room and went into the men's room, following the signs until he came to the shower stalls across from a line of sinks. He shaved first then got into the shower and scrubbed, using the soap in a dispenser on the wall. He was sorry he would have to put the same clothes on again after showering, but there was no way he could afford anything different.

When he popped out of the shower and dried off with a white towel from the courtesy stack, he checked to make sure his clothes and especially his wallet inside were still there. But it was a quiet time, and he had nothing to worry about until he went back outside.

The lights were on in the truck. He could hear its diesel engine going. Even as he watched, it started to move.

Hardy ran as flat-out fast as he could go. The truck was going slow but getting faster as it headed toward the parking lot's exit.

He was panting hard and was afraid the truck was going to get away from him. But a battered pickup truck was crossing the access road, and the yacht-transport truck had to slow slightly.

Hardy raced the last few feet and leaped to grab the back of the truck as it started off onto the access road, heading for the ramp.

He was still climbing the ladder to get into the yacht as the truck pulled out onto the highway. Tempted to lie down and breathe deeply, he went across the deck, unlocked the hatch, and went below. Only then did he go to his knees and gasp until his breathing returned to normal.

How ironic that at one point he had thought of stopping the truck so that he could stay back there in Connecticut, and now he didn't want to lose his ride on the yacht across America.

In a trip out into the Connecticut countryside, he had made a discovery. He'd found tree-lined clear streams with trout hiding behind rocks in the current. Open green pastures and thick stands of green vegetation were a stark contrast to the big cities like Hartford and New Haven. Now, he wanted to see the other states like that, to imagine their hidden and wondrous secrets.

He stowed his shaving kit and brought out his book and flashlight, hoping to read just a bit until he had calmed down enough to get back to sleep.

Before he had even stretched out, he heard a rumble of thunder, and rain began to pound down onto the yacht's deck. Maybe he wouldn't need to read to get to some rest. The inside of the boat was dry and cozy. The sound of the steady rain, even its hammering, he found soothing.

He was slipping the book and light back into his bag when an even harder hammering began to thump steadily on the hatch.

Hardy put his bag in the cabinet and stood as motionless and quiet as he could. He could hear a voice yelling something. It could hardly be the driver. The truck was still moving.

He moved closer to the hatch, listening hard.

"Hardy. Hardy. Open up!" The voice was female. It sounded like a voice he knew.

The hammering and shouting started in again. He didn't know if the driver could hear all the banging, but he sure didn't want him to. He stepped to the hatch and unlocked it. When he opened it, a very wet Ivy Palmer with a foil blanket pulled tight over her head looked down at him. Strands of her wet hair were plastered to her cheeks, and the rain poured off her.

"Get out of the way." She clambered inside, dripping all over the place.

He shut the hatch and locked it. Then he turned to her.

She wore the same clothes he'd last seen her wearing and was clutching a small purse. Ivy tossed the wet blanket aside and reached to brush her damp hair back. With skies the black of night and with the rain outside, the cabin was dimly lit. The occasional sprays of lights from passing vehicles gave the room a flicker now and again, only to settle back into darkness.

"You're probably wondering," she said, "why I'm here."

Chapter 5

One of Hardy's classmates, Whit perhaps, had said of Ivy, "She's so skinny she thinks cottage cheese is a comfort food." Her looks and build didn't bother Hardy a bit. Her folks being old-money rich while he was a low-level employee—that's what made his insides curl up like an earthworm on a hot skillet.

HARDY *was* wondering why and how Ivy was there. Just some of the thoughts cartwheeling through his head were to ponder if she was stalking him or keeping an eye on the boat for her father or any number of other reasons that made less and less sense as he thought of them.

"How you got here at all is the bigger riddle."

"I've been here all along."

"Really?"

"I used the boat's emergency blanket, the kind that folds up to the size of a wallet." She pointed at the dripping foil blanket at their feet. "The label says it's made of polyester designed from the insulation used in space exploration. I used it to explore the space under the Zodiac."

"It couldn't have been comfortable out there."

"It wasn't, most of the time." She reached up to brush back a wet strand of hair. "But I had my moments. I was stretched out on my back, watching the stars go by once. I was trying for that again tonight, but cloud cover obscured everything. Then the skies opened up."

Hardy felt his way across to the cabinet and fetched out his small flashlight from his gym bag.

"If you want to run a comb through your hair, this will get you to the mirror in the head." He turned the light on and handed it to her. "Don't use up the batteries. They're all I have."

"We can get more," she huffed. She snatched the light from him and took off toward the head.

The rain beat down on the boat, but he wasn't able to savor the cozy, protected feeling of being inside any longer. He had just really begun to savor the adventure of being alone too.

She came out of the head, using one of the formerly tightly folded towels to dry her hair, and caught the alarmed look on his face. "I suppose you were trying to keep everything pristine and unused."

Ivy crossed the room to check the one bed in the cabin. "Is this where you've been sleeping?"

"Yeah, but..." He waited for a response. When he got none, he said, "I should be alright on the floor."

She came over to hand him back his flashlight. In the dim light, he could barely make out her face, and the storm hammering and howling around them as the yacht moved through the night only made the moment eerier.

"What are you afraid of with me?"

"Everything."

"You're not gay, are you?"

"No, just cheerful."

He thought her low chuckle was somewhere between a purr and a growl.

"Have you ever even dated before?" she asked.

His head rocked back an inch. Could he tell her about Claire, how he had thought she was the one, only to come back from college in a surprise visit to find that the surprise was on him? She and his best friend, Dave, had sat up in bed, the sheet dropping away from their nude bodies—all this on the mattress Hardy had scrimped to buy her.

And, of the two women with whom he'd ever been intimate, she had been the kinder one.

"Will your parents be looking for you?" he asked.

"I told them I went off on a sudden trip with friends to Europe."

I guess people with money can do that. He thought it but said nothing.

"I know what you're thinking," she said. "The answer is I keep in touch with a phone call a day."

"How do they...?"

"I google the details of different countries, the food, that sort of thing. Right now, I'm in Lisbon. The stuff I'm finding out about it online makes me want to actually go there sometime. What about you?"

"So far, this is the height of my travel experience. But, sure, I'd like to see the world someday."

"Hmm."

"What if they check your room and find you didn't take your passport?"

"First of all, they wouldn't dare enter my room," she said. "Secondly, I take it with me everywhere. You never know."

"I guess I would have thought that taking a sudden trip to Europe would be pretty spontaneous and daring. But I didn't expect to be yachting across America on dry land a few days ago."

"One thing. My phone's battery is dying down. Where can I recharge it?"

"Not in here. All the power is turned off. Plus, your dad had me take out all the water and food supplies, anything heavy."

"How did a conversation about my battery end up on the subject of food?" She tilted her head.

"You'll find it's a subject that comes up when you face several days with little opportunity for fine dining."

"Now you've made me hungry. I haven't had anything other than some cottage cheese."

"So that was you."

"I suppose Dad had you take even the canned food out of the old tub, right?"

He nodded but didn't know if she could make out the gesture in the dim light. "I've got a little bit of food."

He went to the fridge and took out a bottle of water and the package of beef jerky. "Here." He handed her the bottle.

"Oh my gosh, I was thirsty." She grabbed the bottle and lifted it up, drinking down half of it at a go. Then she reached into the bag and took out a piece of jerky.

After chewing for almost a minute, she said, "Oh my. It's like when those starving cowboys had to eat their belts, or something."

He started to fold the top of the bag.

"But it's food." She grabbed for the bag and took out another piece.

"I was kind of pacing myself," he said, "so it would last."

"Okay," she said but took out another piece before she handed the bag back. "It is edible once I've gnawed it into a soup in my mouth."

He shook his head at that mental image as he sealed the package and put it back in the fridge and swung the latch back in place that locked its door so nothing could spill when at sea.

"Is the refrigerator turned on?"

"Nothing's turned on. It just seemed the right place to store food."

"Too bad. I could just about live on cottage cheese, although chewing old belt is fun too." She reached up with a finger to pick a bit of meat from her teeth.

"I didn't see you at the truck stop."

"You weren't supposed to. But I saw you, enough to keep clear. I've got to tell you there was nothing tempting about that women's bathroom there. I kept imagining holes drilled in the walls where someone could watch."

"Were there?"

"Not that I could see, but that doesn't always mean anything."

"It's sure a different world out here."

"There are some harder edges in places," she said. "But look at us. We've survived so far."

"Are you going to tell your father on me?"

"You haven't realized yet that you could as easily tell my father on me. Or that telling on you might blow my cover story." She stepped closer to him.

He nearly took a step back. "You think we can do this, travel together?" he asked. His first thought was *No way*.

"Sure," she said.

He was close enough to see into her eyes. A flash of lightning from outside helped. She didn't seem to be looking at him with eyes that wanted to fall in love but rather with the look of someone who'd been disappointed a time or two.

He'd never let himself look at her so closely before. He took a step back.

"I guess... I guess we should try and get some sleep," he said.

"And you're okay with the floor?"

"I suppose I'll have to be."

"Well, I got by on the hard teak deck with only that foil blanket," she said.

"I'm okay with the floor."

"I knew you would be. That's something about you."

"What do you mean?"

"Girls who like bad boys always, always, always get the opportunity to rue their bias later. I've had several friends who learned that the hard way."

She went over to the bed and climbed onto it.

He went to the cabinet and got his book out of his gym bag. While he was there, he took down a spare blanket that was strapped in place.

In one corner, he spread out her wet foil blanket to dry. Hardy stretched himself out alongside the stairs that led down into the cabin.

He got comfortable on top of half the blanket with the other half around him then turned on his flashlight and flipped to the stretch where Dana was going around Cape Horn in a storm. The passage suited the moment, with the rain still pouring, accompanied by occasional thunder and flashes of lightning outside.

"Are you going to read?"

"Looks that way," he said. That was the last they spoke until morning.

He lifted the book and saw she wasn't looking his way, so he lowered it.

How am I going to get rid of her?

He couldn't very well push her off the side as they rolled along, and he didn't want to just take off himself. He was just starting to really savor seeing America out the porthole windows.

Often when he was finishing up on the cleaning of the yacht, Reginald Palmer would show up, ready to take it out to sea. Sometimes, he would be wearing a suit, from which he would change below into an outfit that made him look like a retired naval officer. With his big lantern jaw and stern look, all he needed was the captain's cap to climb up onto the bridge of a destroyer. But he was usually in a good mood when he came to the boat and congratulated Hardy each time on having the boat Bristol fashion, ready to go. A couple of times, he had hired Hardy for the day to captain the yacht and sail it while he entertained business associates. He treated Hardy well, but they had never been what Hardy would call pals.

Sometimes, Ivy would be along with him, in shorts and deck shoes, ready to sail. At first, she had ignored him, acted like Hardy was invisible in his cutoff denim shorts, T-shirt beginning to sprout holes, and hands callused from working the decks and getting the trim to a shine.

Then something had changed. She began to notice him, even called out his name when asking permission to come aboard. Her father picked up on the flirtish lilt, the first time swinging his head toward

Hardy in a brief forbidding glare. But he must have realized the boy wasn't doing anything—it was all Ivy. He'd shaken that big head and gone on with his inspection of the craft.

In all the time Hardy had worked for Reginald Palmer, he had never gotten the kind of condescending looks and tone he had recognized from others, the more than a hint that he was but a poor boy and they were a better class of people. He didn't himself see the cleaning and maintaining of the yacht as demeaning. It had been honest, hard work for a wage he earned. Yet he never shook the sense that Palmer was his employer, that he came from old money, and that his daughter was off limits.

Ivy began to pop up in several places, at school even though it wasn't the one she attended, at the gym, and more often when he was working up a sweat while cleaning the yacht, stocking supplies, and getting fresh water and fuel for the generator. Her perky face would be smiling, eager, and more than a little mischievous. If she had been anyone else, he might have been flattered, interested. Egalitarian that he was, that shouldn't have mattered. He wasn't sure how he felt when she would come around, except the opposite of relaxed.

Ah, well. He lifted the book again. When he tried to read, the words on the page blurred. He could feel and hear his own heart beating. Nothing felt the same. He turned off his light and lay there thinking. Was his trip, his adventure, spoiled? Most of all, he wondered if they could get along or how long it might be before she might want more. In the dark, his thoughts swirled around and around. The storm raged with growing intensity outside as the yacht moved on through the night.

Chapter 6

Blackbeard, the pirate formerly known as Edward Teach, knew how to evoke fear. He would light slow cannon matches in his beard so a demonic cloud of smoke surrounded his glaring face on his towering frame and his eponymic full black beard, making him look like the devil himself as he swung by rope onto the deck in a cameo appearance in Hardy's brief middle-of-the-night dream. On a ship at sea. That's why, *he thought for part of a second then went back to sleep.*

HARDY WOKE, STRETCHED his arms, and realized without opening his eyes that he was on the floor. The sound of the storm was gone, replaced by the steady whir of the truck's tires on asphalt.

Waking was always the best time of any day. It was like being born, new and fresh again—

for a short time having no memory of anything bad happening. Yet memories did eventually wriggle into place.

He recalled how he used to lie on his cot, one of eight in the boys' crowded upstairs room at the Sandersons' makeshift orphanage, awake but reluctant to open his eyes, knowing they would be shouted up in just a minute or two. He could smell the bacon and eggs they were making for themselves and the oatmeal that he and the other children would get.

He had learned in time that they were paid for the number of children in their care and that most of the money and food they kept for themselves. One Christmas morning, he sneaked from his unheated upstairs sleeping quarters to look down into the living room. Mr. Sanderson and Mrs. Sanderson were taking away most of the presents the local charities had brought for the orphans. He saw them take money from the hand of the man taking away the presents.

From his drowsy, contemplative half-awake state, he went from feeling and hearing the low growl of the tires on the road to being fully awake. His eyes snapped all the way open. He had company on the yacht now. *Oh no!*

His thoughts went back to the options: push her off the side or slip away himself.

The bed was empty. She sat looking out the porthole at more green hills rolling by. The sun was bright, and any sign of the storm was long gone.

"I helped myself to one of your water bottles," she said, "but I wasn't up to eating more cowboy belt for breakfast. Maybe the driver will stop for breakfast or something."

Hardy reached up to rub at the fuzz on his chin, awkward and way too self-aware.

She rose and went over to the other side. "It's like being on a train, only without a dining car."

"Hard not to think about food now and then, isn't it?"

"I'm kind of used to that, but I wouldn't say no to a nice cup of hot tea when the flight attendant comes around."

"It would be a steward. You were on the train metaphor, remember?"

"That's right, while in a yacht pulled by a truck. Hard to keep it all straight."

He went to the fridge, being as quiet as he could.

"Hey," she said, "you don't need to tiptoe about on my behalf. It may be my father's boat, but you were the first one on board in this swashbuckler of an adventure. Pirate rules apply."

"Okay, then."

He took out one of the water bottles as well as one piece of jerky. He stayed at the fridge to nibble at the end of the jerky so she wouldn't see him gnawing away like some sort of caveman.

"Hey, come look at this lot," she said. "I wonder where they're headed, packed tight the way they are."

Hardy went over to crowd close beside her to look out the porthole. An SUV cruised by. He could see at least six people inside and four dogs. The side window of the back seat was open on this side, and all four dogs had their heads out, sniffing at the air that tugged at their ears and open mouths.

Their happy eagerness gave Hardy a tickle of joy. Ivy was grinning as well. She made no move to get closer to him and seemed comfortable just looking out at the world as he had been doing.

"Didn't you get to look around when you were topside?" he asked.

"I took a few peeks, but I had to stay hunkered down for the most part, stretching out the day into a series of naps. This is far better, being in here where no one can see us and we can savor the world."

He gave her a quick sideways glance. He realized how tense he had been all morning, careful of everything he said.

"We're changing highways." Hardy watched the highway signs. "I think we're heading southwest this time."

"That makes sense. We're headed for San Diego." She came over to look out his porthole at the signs they passed. "There were lots of places earlier where the roads led to a more southern route."

"I suppose a guy in this business has driven back and forth from coast to coast quite a few times. He may have his own preferred route."

"Well, I'm glad he changed highways. There's a bit more to see on this one."

They passed a town in the distance where they could see a Ferris wheel going around. A bit farther along, they saw a cleanly mowed field near a set of red barns surrounded by what looked like giant white marshmallows.

"Must be some sort of protective covering for bales of something," she said. "I saw one yellow sign for Amish people a while back, but I haven't seen a single horse and carriage."

"We probably won't, out here on the highway, though I would fancy seeing a horse that could pull a carriage along at over sixty miles an hour."

"The horse would have to be Pegasus," she said. "Then I'd like to see that, too, with some Amish guy in the carriage with his hair pulled back by the wind like ZZ Top."

They switched from side to side, getting excited at each new wonder. She glanced toward the boat's head a couple of times and finally said, "I hope we stop sometime soon."

"He's been driving for a while. We probably need fuel, if nothing else."

As if he'd heard them, the truck took an exit ramp after only a few more miles.

While the driver fueled the truck, Ivy climbed down and kept to the other side of the truck and trailer to scurry off toward the convenience store's bathrooms.

Hardy listened long enough to ensure the driver was still busy. He ran off, too, toward the men's bathroom inside. He hoped the driver would pause for breakfast, but he didn't want to take the chance. So he washed his face quickly, ran his wet fingers through his hair, and looked at the stubble on his face and wished he could shave. He shook his head and headed back toward the yacht, making sure the driver couldn't see him.

He was up the back and on the deck when he heard the driver come around and start up the back of the truck and then up the stairs at the yacht's stern. He shot down inside the cabin and locked it. Seconds later, he heard the driver walk the deck and give the hatch a tug. *Whew!*

The driver climbed back down. In a few moments, the truck started up in a coughing rumble.

Hardy unlocked the hatch and went up onto the deck. He could see Ivy running, a bag flapping in one hand. The truck began to move.

The driver was usually slow and steady, but the truck began to roll across the lot toward the exit. Ivy ran faster.

Without a thought, Hardy climbed down onto the back of the truck and extended an arm.

Ivy's eyes were open wide. The last few yards the moving truck made, she gave a frantic burst of pumping legs. She reached and grabbed at Hardy's hand. He caught her wrist while she grasped his. He pulled her up and held her to the truck until she had a firm grip.

Now why did I do that?

The opportunity to be alone on his trip again had come and gone so quickly it had been a blur of a wink. Yet he felt more puzzled than disappointed. *Why?*

Chapter 7

Hardy let Ivy climb up first. He was still getting onto the deck as the truck moved along the access road and started up the ramp to the highway.

They clambered below and shut the hatch.

She was panting hard. "I thought we had more time than we did. I tried for a quick sink bath."

"I'm glad you made it."

She tilted her head at him. "I do believe you mean that."

"I do." And he did, but damned if he knew why.

She held up the bag she'd carried from the store. "I got you more of your beloved cowboy belt." She pulled a package of beefy jerky out of the bag, the same brand he'd purchased before.

"And for you?"

"They didn't have cottage cheese. I got some sort of bottled yogurt smoothie shake. It's green because it has lots of kale in it."

"Yum."

"I picked up a box of granola bars, too, something even you might be able to eat."

For the rest of the day, they were like two kids on a school outing or picnic. They watched out the portholes as dusk settled around them and the sky gradually grew dark.

"I haven't figured out this driver's system yet," Hardy said. "He's slow and conservative in general. Sometimes, he stops and rests when night comes. Other times, he seems to roll on through the dark."

After a while, they could only look at lights in the distance on the starboard side. All they could see of the cars that passed them to the port side were their headlight beams. So they went back and sat on the side next to each other, seeing what little they could through the dark.

Ivy yawned. "If you don't mind..."

"No. I'm with you. And you had a more harrowing day than me, besides."

"Nobody said a pirate's life is easy."

He went over to the cabinet, took out his blanket, and unfolded it as a bed on the floor.

She was up on the bed by the time he got out his book and flashlight.

"If you're going to read anyway, maybe you can read to me for a while."

"Okay." He tried to think of which part might hold her interest—certainly not the flogging scene. He liked the passage up the coast and the islands once the *Pilgrim* was off California. But she wouldn't have much context for that. So he started at the beginning, with Dana stepping away from his undergraduate days at Harvard to go to sea, the clothes he put together for the trip, and his first impressions as the ship departed.

He read on as the yacht rolled along behind the truck through the night. Just as he got to the part where Dana was about to make it through his only bout of seasickness, Hardy looked down and saw that Ivy was asleep.

He stood up and shook one leg that was trying to go asleep. Outside the nearest porthole, he looked up at the black sky and could make out a lopsided moon. He went over to his spot on the floor and curled up with the blanket around him. He flipped ahead to when it was Easter Sunday and Dana had shore leave and he and a friend hired horses and rode them up and down the hard sand beaches in the sea-salt breeze.

A short while later, he turned off the light, put the book on the floor, and eased off to sleep.

THE TRUCK WAS STILL rolling along as the sun began to come up.

"He was really a goer for this leg of the trip," Hardy said as he rose and stretched. "Maybe it's like a horse smelling the barn and knowing it's nearing home."

"We're a far sight from being near San Diego," Ivy said. "Maybe you can give me a hand with this bed. I can't get it nearly as taut as you always kept it."

He stowed his blanket, book, and light. Then he made short work of making the bed tight enough an army sergeant could have bounced a quarter off it and would have been pleased.

They both looked restlessly about, probably thinking about the same thing, a bathroom.

Their hopes lifted as the truck slowed for a ramp. Hardy said, "Hey, he's getting off here. But I don't see a roadside rest or truck stop."

"Hard to believe he wants to do a little back-road slumming."

"Well, this is sure different. We're getting to see some real nooks and crannies of America now."

The road got smaller, and the boat passed under wires low enough it couldn't have gotten through with its masts up. The houses that went by varied widely, from three-bedroom ranch homes to trailers up on blocks. At last, the truck came to a slow stop at an intersection with an even smaller road.

The engine idled. The driver seemed to be waiting for something. Hardy couldn't imagine what. He looked around at some scruffy growth and one burned-out trailer with nothing but twisted black metal sheets of siding scattered in piles on the ground like big black chips.

The truck idled. They waited.

After a while, two small children came out to the corner. They stood waiting. Barely five minutes later, a yellow school bus pulled up and opened its door. They climbed up inside, and the bus pulled away.

The truck shifted into gear and turned the corner, heading back down the lane to a white house with flaking paint that was flanked by a barn that had once been a brighter red.

The driver turned the truck around so it was facing out. He turned off the engine. A woman came out of the house. She wore a red-checked apron over a blue summer dress.

The driver carried a small travel bag in one hand and met her halfway. They embraced.

"His wife?" Ivy asked.

"I don't think so. He waited on those kids to leave before he went to the house. A father would have wanted to see his kids. Maybe a single parent?"

"Or a married one, and our guy is something of a rake." She stared at the closed front door of the house. "I sure wish he'd made a rest stop instead. I guess there's no way we could use the bathroom."

"It's a country place. Look over by the barn. See the smaller wooden building?"

"An outhouse. You want me to use an outhouse."

"It's that or the woods, and there's not much of a woods." Only a few trees around the house and barn had been spared when someone cleared the land.

"Well, if I must." She went to the head and came out carrying a roll of toilet paper. "Like as not, there's only an old Sears catalog hanging by a rope for you to tear out pages to use."

"You seem to know more than you let on about country ways."

"Oh, sure. I slip out into the countryside every now and again to let out a yodel."

She opened the hatch and started up onto the deck.

"Don't let them see you."

She gave him a curt wave with one hand without looking back.

Hardy had nearly told her about the only time he'd ever been in an old-time outhouse before. Someone had written on the wall, "Anything over ten pounds must be lowered with a rope." He had decided that was just the sort of thing that was not likely to inform, entertain, or in any way amuse her. His holding back made him wonder if her opinion of him was starting to matter.

He watched her go across the open dirt of the yard, bent low and scampering from one scrap of cover to the next. Her furtive moves probably drew more attention than if she had calmly walked across the open space to the barn. Hardy had a suspicion, though, that the driver was too busy to be looking outside, and the woman as well.

The noises outside were sure different in the country setting where they were parked. Instead of truck doors slamming and the low hum of men talking in a truck stop parking lot, a rooster insisted on crowing again and again even though the sun had long ago risen. Later, some sort of canine howled in the distance—a dog, Hardy hoped, and not a coyote. Closer he heard the *baa, baa* of goats, ones he could see grazing except for one that stood on top of an overturned wheelbarrow.

"I wonder how long we'll be stuck out here in the wilderness," she said as she came back down into the cabin.

"My hunch is that he will be off like a speckled bird before those kids come home from school." He held up a hand. "My turn in the luxury bathroom accommodations."

"You won't call it luxury once you've been inside. Just a heads-up: there's a small nest of wasps in one corner you might keep an eye on. I don't think the family uses the outhouse anymore, but they keep the thing around as some sort of reminder."

"Not a reminder of happier days, I'm guessing." Hardy started up the stairs.

On his way back to the yacht, he looped around and passed through the barn. The animal stalls were all empty, and what hay was left in the loft looked dried and stale.

As he climbed back inside the yacht, he saw Ivy shaking her head. She held up her cell phone. "I'm in Barcelona now. But I'm about out of power, so I had to cut the world-tour description short. I never lied to my parents before, never needed to. But it's kind of fun."

"I saw an outlet in the barn. If you hurry, you might be able to rustle up enough of a charge to get you the rest of the way across Europe."

"We *are* pirates," she said as she headed for the stairs. "That makes me wonder where the word *buccaneer* came from. Out in these parts, it probably relates to corn. You know, a buck an ear."

"I believe one version says it came from the French word *boucan*, a grill used in the Caribbean for cooking and curing dried meat for use on the ships. Since the pirates on the old Spanish Main did the same thing, the word started to be used for them as well."

She paused on the ladder, looked like she wanted to say something, but shook her head and started to go out the hatch. She stopped again and looked back at him.

"Did you spout this sort of thing a lot when you were in school?"

"Well, yeah, I guess I did."

"Okay. Now, I'm beginning to understand why those guys wanted to beat you up." She went on out the hatch.

Hardy guessed that the driver would head back for the truck before a school bus dropped the kids off at the end of the lane.

Ivy was back inside long before then. They left the hatch ajar for as long as they dared to catch what bit of breeze they could to keep the cabin cool. They were only partially successful since the sun was beating down.

"Time to close the hatch and lock it," Hardy said. "Here he comes."

They both peeked out the porthole. The driver had been wearing an orange shirt when he went in. He had switched to a blue check shirt.

"He must have bathed," Ivy said. "Blast him."

The driver lowered the bag he carried to the ground. They watched him come to climb up and check that the top of the yacht was still secure. He checked the hatch. Then he climbed down and went around and started the truck's engine.

In his characteristic slow and careful way, he started up the lane to get them back on the highway.

Abruptly, the truck slowed to a stop.

"Now what?" Ivy went to the porthole to look outside. "Oh."

"What is it?" Hardy came up beside her and leaned close until their shoulders touched.

The truck had stopped beside the burned-out double-wide trailer they had seen earlier. In the yard, a black dog slowly lifted its head to look their way. As it got slowly to its feet, Hardy could see its ribs. A chain led all the way to the nearby tree with its trunk also blackened on one side from whatever fire had reduced the trailer to a dark pile of rubble.

"Oh my. Someone has just left that poor chained-up dog there to die."

The driver approached the dog slowly and waited until he got a slow, tired wag from its tail. Then he reached down and undid the chain from where it fastened to the dog's collar.

"Well, good for him," Ivy said.

The driver left the dog in the black-singed yard and started back for the truck. The dog tried to follow him, going slowly because of a slight limp.

"Oh, Hardy. Look at him."

Hardy had already started up the stairs to open the hatch and race across the deck. He climbed down to the ground just as the truck started to move again.

The limping dog was trying to catch up but was falling behind.

Hardy scooped up the dog, which felt far lighter than he had expected. He began to run after the truck.

Ivy climbed down until she could reach out. Hardy handed the dog up to her and leaped to grab onto the back of the truck just as its speed picked up.

Still on the deck of the moving yacht, they checked the dog over. The dog lifted his right front paw. Hardy felt between the pads and found a spiky grass burr. He picked it out and threw it out behind the truck. He checked, and the other paws were okay, no burrs there. Up close, he could see the old black dog was mostly lab, with a white muzzle and rheumy eyes. He licked at their hands, and his tail managed a couple more wags.

Hardy looked up at Ivy. She was wiping at her eyes. "Let's take him below," he said.

Chapter 8

Catching Hardy reading a library book on ancient history, studying when he was supposed to be doing chores at the orphanage, Mr. Sanderson shook his head. "Read all you want, but you'll always be a bumpkin. The thing about doing well at school is that you can still be quite naïve about life. It's going to take someone like you all your life to ever really know anything that matters."

Hardy had looked up at him. "That's okay. I have that much time."

"HE NEEDS FOR US TO give him a bath," Ivy said. "The recent rain must have done part of the job for us. But he still needs a real bath. There's also no name tag on his collar."

Hardy brought over a bowl from the galley, along with a bottle of water. He poured some water into the bowl and slid it close to the dog's head.

The dog lay on the floor, pressed against one of Ivy's legs. He rose to his feet and put his head to the bowl and lapped away. When he finally stopped, licking at his white muzzle as he looked up at them, the bowl was almost empty.

"Man, he sure was thirsty," she said.

"I'll bet he's hungry too." Hardy went to the fridge and brought back three pieces of beef jerky. "Don't give him too much at once. We need to tear the pieces into smaller ones. We don't want him to choke."

The dog grabbed at the first small piece Hardy held out to him. He barely chewed before he gulped it down. His eyes fixed on Hardy's hands until another piece was near his mouth. He grabbed at it, chewing more slowly this time, savoring it. Hardy let Ivy feed him the rest of the jerky she held. His tail wagged as vigorously as it had yet, and his rheumy, watery eyes shifted from one to the other of them.

"Let's call him Frosty," she said.

"He's mostly a black dog, not white."

"His nose and face are white."

"Okay with me. Frosty it is."

The dog looked around for anything more to eat then lowered his head and finished off the rest of the water in the bowl.

Hardy poured the rest of the water from the bottle into the bowl.

"Now that we have a dog," she said, "maybe you should be reading *Travels with Charley*."

"We're still on a boat. Dana will get us through." He went over to look out the porthole just in time to see open pastures surrounded by fences below the highway, sprawling off to a line of trees.

Next, green wooded hills rose up from the side of the road. Frosty came over to lay his head on Hardy's thigh.

"Oh my," Ivy said. She looked out the other side's porthole.

"What is it?"

"You'd better come look."

The truck had slowed to a near crawl.

Flashing red and blue lights swirled on two state trooper vehicles blocking a lane of traffic. An SUV was overturned in the grassy median strip. An ambulance had pulled up close, and its emergency medical people were pulling two bloodied people out of the vehicle. But at least they were able to stand.

His stomach gave a lurch. He looked away.

"What's the matter?" Ivy asked.

"As long as I can remember, I can't watch a motorcycle crash or anyone falling hard off a skateboard on TV without feeling a punch of their pain myself."

"Wow. I'd say you have a heightened sense of empathy. Does it bother you when you're doing your martial arts thingy?"

"No. My thingy is okay when actively defending myself. I did break a couple of collarbones one year. I felt bad about that."

"Did you heal quickly?"

"Well, they weren't *my* collarbones. The point was I felt bad later for hurting anyone. I usually seek to come out ahead but with minimal long-term damage to others."

"Except their pride."

"Usually, their pride needed a friendly spanking."

"Like those guys from your school?"

"They got off easy."

Ivy kept looking out the window, but with a pensive stare, as if not seeing much for a moment or two. "I guess having too much empathy is a good thing, just one of your little quirks."

"Better than the other extreme, where seeing people getting badly hurt makes me laugh. That would mean I was more like a psychopath. Just being a little quirky is better than that."

"We're all a little quirky. It's what makes us interesting." She turned to him, her normally smooth forehead furrowed by a couple of wrinkle lines.

Frosty wriggled between them and wagged his tail as he looked up at them.

Ivy rubbed the dog's head and scratched him behind the ears. Frosty tilted his head back and half closed his eyes. "So you're a therapy dog, too, are you?" He wagged his tail harder.

Much of the highway travel for a spell was just routine highway. They could see towns in the distance as they passed them. The family shows in the cars going by sometimes held surprises. One had a dog's head out every window except the driver's side. She was the only human inside.

In another SUV, a family was transfixed by a movie showing while the driver took them through real America if they would just look out their windows.

As the truck climbed the slow grade of a steeper hill, they could look over the top of a tall metal fence to see hundreds and hundreds of wrecked vehicles, many turning orange with rust and no doubt heating up in the blaze of the sun.

"Ugh," Ivy said, rubbing at Frosty's ears.

"I imagine there's more of that sort of thing to see than we know, along with fast-food joints, seamy night spots, and strip mall after strip mall wanting to sell, sell, sell."

"Well, they're going to have to get someone other than us to buy, buy, buy," Ivy said.

Hardy sighed in relief when the truck finally pulled off the highway down a ramp and into a truck stop.

"Let's be careful this time," Ivy said. "Our driver may have done this route numerous times as he's hauled boats back and forth across the country, but he's shown no consistent pattern, and that includes at least one pit stop where I think he was getting busy."

"He was getting something," Hardy agreed. "But he's pulling up to a parking spot and not the pumps. Let's see where he goes."

They waited and were finally rewarded with seeing the driver's blue shirt heading toward the restaurant.

"I wouldn't mind having the plate of bacon and eggs with hash browns he's probably going to order," Hardy said.

"Maybe you could sneak an order to go."

He thought of his dwindling wallet contents. "Naw. I still have some jerky left that Frosty hasn't eaten."

They had time for a quick clean-up each in the restrooms. Hardy had a ten-minute shower and shave, brushed his teeth quickly, then went outside the convenience store to wait on Ivy.

She saw he held his shaving kit when she came up to him. "You'd better not carry that inside. I'll pick up a few things and meet you back at the boat."

He couldn't fault her for taking long to shop. Less than fifteen minutes later, she was coming down into the cabin and locking the hatch behind her.

She held up the bag she carried. "I was able to get four cans of Alpo. Guess who they're for?"

"Not me, I hope," Hardy said.

Almost an hour later, the driver climbed up to check that the hatch was locked and the deck looked okay. Frosty let out a low rumble of a growl from deep in his throat. Ivy reached over to hold a hand on his muzzle until the driver's footsteps moved away and he climbed down from the yacht.

"Good catch," Hardy said. "I'm glad the old fellow isn't a barker."

"He's more the silent type," she said. "I like that."

Hardy thought about that for a minute or two longer than he should have, wondering if that was also about himself and if it was a compliment or if he'd been talking too much.

As they switched back and forth from one porthole to the other to watch everything going by, Frosty moved with them, not wanting to be far from them.

"Separation anxiety," Ivy said.

Hardy nodded.

A family's camper passed them on the left.

Ivy turned to Hardy. "It would be swell if we could stop and sample some of the countryside diners, taste the sort of food each area specializes in cooking."

"You would just get cottage cheese or something."

"I was thinking of you."

"Well, I guess I know what you mean. It would be nice if we could pull off the road if we wanted to see the giant ball of string or look around inside a cavern or paddle kayaks down a stream."

"Maybe when this little adventure jaunt is over, we can take the other kind of trip someday."

"Maybe," he said. He had a hard time thinking about the future or the past. Someone had told him that dogs live in the "now." That was how he'd felt about the whole trip so far, with an added touch of surreal when Ivy had revealed she was on the yacht too.

The driver kept up his usual speed limit pace and didn't seem to be pushing himself or his load. At dusk, as the sky was showing a ripple of pink and purple of the setting sun ahead of them to the west, he eased into a roadside rest and parked behind an eighteen-wheeler. A string of them lined the sides of the ramps going in and out of the rest stop.

He left the engine running. They watched him cross to the bathroom and come back several minutes later. The truck's cab door closed, and he probably climbed into his sleeping compartment.

"At least we have bathrooms." He petted Frosty's head as he looked out the porthole.

Not too many of the drivers were coming and going to the bathrooms, and no one was going to the ladies' side just then.

"But no showers."

"We can briefly walk Frosty."

Hardy knew where some spare rope was stowed. He used a knife from the galley to cut the right length. Ivy watched him splice a loop for a handle and then a slip-knot noose to go around Frosty's neck.

"You're pretty handy with knots," she said.

"I hope you're not reading anything kinky into that."

"Trust me. My thoughts are far from kinky."

They led Frosty to the stern of the yacht's deck. Hardy climbed down the back of the truck. Frosty was still light enough Ivy could hand him down to him.

Frosty's tail wagged vigorously. He stopped to sniff at just about everything. Frosty was quite the sniffer. When he found just the place he wanted, he did his business. Hardy took out the plastic bag he'd stuffed into one pocket and cleaned up after the dog. He got rid of that at the next trash barrel they passed.

Ivy waited at the back of the boat and helped him get the dog back up.

"It's a good thing we stopped when we did. He was ready for a bathroom break." He nodded toward the restrooms. "You go first."

When she came back, she said, "There's a faucet behind the restrooms." She went to a cabinet and took out a towel.

"I was being careful about not using those towels."

"I'm sure Dad won't mind. It's for a good cause." She reminded him, as she said it, that she was the owner's daughter. It made him feel more the hired hand and stowaway than ever.

They got the dog down from the boat once more and led him around to the back of the restrooms. There wasn't as much light there. Hardy thought that was a good thing. He supposed washing a dog wasn't that unusual an event, and even if their truck's driver saw them, he still didn't know who they were or how they got there.

Hardy turned the water on to a trickle and began to wet down the dog, who thought it fun. He twisted his rump and wagged his tail. The concrete sloped enough so that the water ran off into the grass. Ivy came around to the back after visiting the ladies' room. She had two handfuls of liquid soap, which she started to rub onto Frosty's back.

Together, they scrubbed at the dog with the soap then rinsed him thoroughly. Hardy couldn't see dirt flowing away in the dim light, but the fur and skin felt cleaner to his touch.

Frosty started to shake off the water, and Ivy got the towel around him almost in time. But they both got sprayed.

Feeling his damp shirt cling to him reminded Hardy he had a limited amount of clothes. But Ivy had less, and she'd been wearing the same clothes the whole time too. Maybe they *were* turning into crusty pirates at sea.

Ivy rubbed the towel over Frosty, who squirmed in joy.

The dog was still slightly damp as they got him back up to the yacht's deck.

When they were below, with the hatch locked, Hardy went over to the cabinet and took out his gym bag. "I've got one clean, dry shirt here."

"What about you?" she asked.

He couldn't see her clearly as she moved about in the dim light, and he could only see a spot of white for Frosty's face.

"I've got my gym T-shirt and shorts." He stripped off his shirt and hung it from a peg by the galley.

"Let me have the dry shirt," she said. "My pants are damp too."

"You can use the shorts if you want, though they're probably big for you."

"Well, aren't you sweet."

He could hear her rustling away as she changed clothes inside the head they couldn't use. Then she came out and got onto the bed.

"Let's pick up on the *Pilgrim*'s adventures at sea tomorrow night, okay? I like to hear you reading to me, but I'm tuckered tonight."

"Me too," he said, though they'd only washed a dog. But he stretched out his blanket on the floor and got onto it. Frosty didn't seem to mind the hard floor and snuggled close to him.

As he started to doze off, with the still slightly damp Frosty pressed against his back on the floor, spooning him, he thought of the way Ivy had earlier said, "Now that *we* have a dog." He stared into the dark with Frosty's breath puffing against his ear. "We," she had said.

The truck started up while it was still dark.

"It's hard to get used to the rhythms of this driver," Ivy said, her voice carrying in the dark.

"I imagine full-time semi-rig drivers go hell for leather most of the time until they need to collapse into a rest," Hardy said. Frosty squirmed behind him. "This guy seems to more or less amble his way. But he does do everything on his terms, and probably wisely. There's a lot less traffic at this hour."

"But less for us to see out the windows," she said.

"Do you think we should tell him we're back here so he could take that into consideration?"

"Oh, go back to sleep." She was quiet after that.

Hardy stayed quiet, too, but not Frosty. He had a slight snore when up close.

Chapter 9

"Feel how soft and fluffy his fur is today." Ivy rubbed at the hair on Frosty's neck and back, giving his rump special attention with a deep scratching that made the tail go back and forth like an up-beat metronome.

Hardy was straightening out the inside of the yacht out of habit. He wished he could wash Frosty's food and water bowls. Perhaps he would at the next stop they made. He would have a small bag of trash to get rid of at that time too. With all the dashing to and from the truck at such places, he was glad they hadn't been spotted by the driver yet or at least linked to riding inside the yacht.

"Oh, look."

Hardy went over to the porthole where she was pointing out. A long stretch of white horse fence abruptly turned to dark-brown horse fence where the property lines shifted. Beyond the brown fence, thirty or more horses were grazing on lush green gently rolling pasture land. A white barn and stable with dark roofs stood beside a two-story house with a row of white pillars along the front porch.

"Well, we certainly know we're in Kentucky if we didn't know before," he said.

Each state he'd seen so far seemed to culture a brand for itself where it could. West Virginia had differed from Pennsylvania. Connecticut was worlds apart from Kentucky, for the most part. But there were sometimes stretches on a big interstate highway, particularly when passing near metropolitan areas, where everything began to look the same.

He could drop that chunk of the state into any other state and not know the difference. Such were the insights of travel.

"You're pretty pensive. What are you thinking about?" she asked.

"Here's the thing about travel, for us anyway. It has its joys, but it's kind of mundane sometimes too. We have to find meals and bathrooms. Not all of it is glamorous. But once in a while, we do find a moment that glitters. That's worth it all. I guess we should dwell on that."

"I suppose it can be pretty much like that on any trip, whether flying first-class or on some cruise ship. There are always off moments. Just think, if you got your wish and got to sail the way Dana did, you would be climbing up and down ropes in a hailstorm with tar on your bare feet."

He chuckled. "I guess I wouldn't care for having tar on my feet or sleeping in a forecastle with other men crowded in close."

"We do have lots of room, even with a dog on board. But it would be nice if the amenities were functional too." She glanced toward the head.

They both breathed a sigh when the truck slowed and started down a ramp toward another truck stop.

They patiently waited until the driver was out of sight. Hardy even clambered down to follow and make sure the driver went into the restaurant. That gave them at least an hour, usually.

Ivy helped get Frosty down, and Hardy let her walk him while he got rid of their accumulated trash in a container outside the convenience store.

Inside the store, he got another twelve-pack of water and four more cans of dog food. He glanced wistfully at the other food as he went by and something smelled good, like barbeque, as he got near the checkout counter. But the diet his wallet was on had made it thin. He would get by on what jerky remained out in the boat.

Back at the truck, they worked as a team, getting the supplies and Frosty back up into the boat.

Then Ivy grabbed her purse. "My turn for a quick shower."

She took off at a run. Hardy got his shaving kit and headed toward the men's restroom.

A couple of truckers who hadn't seen each other in a spell were yelling back and forth inside. One or two more came inside and as quickly went back out as soon as they were done. None of them paid any attention to Hardy. Grabbing a quick shave in a truck stop restroom was too commonplace for that.

He was waiting outside the convenience store when Ivy came up to him, her blond hair still damp enough to look almost brunette. The look emphasized her oversized hazel eyes.

She grinned at him. "You'd better wait out here while I get a few things. You can't carry that in there." She nodded toward his shaving kit.

He imagined folks had carried in a whole lot worse, but perhaps she wanted to purchase something she didn't want him to see.

She came out a few minutes later, and her fine hair was already beginning to dry and regain its wispy blondness. The wind lifted a strand and dropped it across her face. She reached up to tuck the wayward strand back in place.

The plastic bag she carried looked bigger than usual, and he thought he smelled something good.

As they walked past the row of gas pumps, he saw two big Harley hog motorcycles beside one row of pumps. No one was near them.

Two very large tattooed guys in denim were crowding in on a biker at another pump. His bike was all black and looked sleek and fast. His outfit matched, also in black, as was the helmet that hung from one handlebar.

One of the big guys yelled something and pushed at the slim biker with a neatly trimmed red beard. Both of the bigger bikers also had beards—large, long, and unmanaged ones.

Hardy handed his shaving kit to Ivy. "You'd better get in the boat."

"You don't have to help."

"Yes, I do."

He heard one of the guys cussing loudly about a rice rocket as he walked closer. Then he shoved the smaller biker in the chest. The other guy stepped in and shoved him too. They looked to be trying to start a fight.

"Hey, what's going on here?" Hardy called out.

"You better butt out, midget. You better just butterscotch outta here. This is none of your affair."

"It's none of mine either," the guy with the red beard said.

A thick arm shot out, and a hand grabbed him by the throat, lifting him off the ground. As he stepped in, Hardy saw a tattoo on the aggressive biker's forearm that showed a grim reaper with a skull face and red gown, holding a scythe. Above the artwork, the tattoo read Grim Reapers MC and said Forever below.

Neither of the two big fellows wore the distinctive biker gang jackets, but Hardy figured them for members of the same club. Both had big beer-drinking bellies and were well over two hundred pounds. One's beard was long, black, and shaggy. The other had nearly the same sort of unmanaged beard in pure white.

"Let go of him!" Hardy yelled. He looked around, but no one seemed eager to come and help.

When Hardy stepped in, the big black-bearded guy swung the back of his hand at Hardy, swatting at him like he was small, pesky fly.

"It's like you're giving me the arm," Hardy muttered to himself.

He grabbed the wrist tightly and yanked while twisting his whole body, ducking under the arm, then standing to twist harder.

Black Beard let go of the guy's neck and tried to hit at Hardy with his fist, though he had to swing across his own twisted body to try. Hardy twisted harder and bent the arm down, squeezing his fingers and thumb on the hand's pressure points. The big guy went all the way up onto his toes, trying to get away. His eyes opened widely, showing fear for the first time. He was very close to getting his arm broken.

White Beard pulled a flip knife from his back pocket and snapped it open and locked the blade into place. He tried to lunge at Hardy, who kept the other man's body between them. Hardy had the man's arm he held twisted up behind his back and had a grip on his other shoulder so he could steer him. Every time the man with the knife would try to step around, Hardy used the other biker as a shield.

The guy who'd been the subject of their abuse tried to step in to help Hardy.

"Don't get cut!" Hardy shouted to him.

When Hardy swung his guy around the next time to avoid the knife, the slim guy with the red beard kicked like he was going for a fifty-yard field goal. He must have connected where he wanted because the guy in Hardy's arms went limp and dropped to his knees while letting out a loud gasp of air.

At the opening, White Beard lunged forward with the knife held high and aimed at Hardy's neck.

Hardy grabbed the wrist and used the guy's momentum and all of his own weight to twist hard.

The guy let go of the knife, which clattered to the asphalt, and he stumbled over his own sidekick. Off balance, he started to fall and grabbed at Hardy as he did.

As he fell and rolled onto his back, all of Hardy's training kicked in. He fell with the biker and grabbed the man's forearm with both hands so his wrist was upward. With his knees bent and with his left leg over the man's neck and his other leg over the bulge of his waist, he pulled the guy's arm while squeezing his legs tight to the body.

Using the guy's chest as a fulcrum, he pulled the man's wrist tighter to his own chest and applied upward pressure from his hips while pulling the hand toward his own chest in the direction of his pinky finger. Once he had the arm bar effectively in place, the guy's other arm was useless, and he began to scream, "You're breaking my arm! You're gonna break the damned arm!"

For the first time, Hardy heard steps pounding their way. He looked around. Three big truckers and what looked like one of the convenience store clerks were running their way.

Hardy let go of his submission hold on the guy and got to his feet.

White Beard shook his arm as he rose and used his other hand to pull the other biker to his feet. They took off in a stumbling run to their bikes, one holding his crotch, the other with a hand to his shoulder. Each got on his Harley and fired it up. They were off in a rumbling roar by the time the other men coming as a posse had arrived.

"You okay?" the clerk asked Hardy, who was brushing off his jeans. "I have it on a security tape. These guys have done this before. They pick a fight, and when the loser gets up later, he finds his wallet is missing."

The truckers were watching the bikes shoot up the ramp. One of them said, "I seriously doubt they were expecting that kind of resistance."

They turned and headed back to their rigs.

"I gotta go too," the clerk said.

When it was just the two of them, the guy with the red beard held out a hand to Hardy. "Thanks. My name's Max Sanders. Those guys were motorcycle gang members, Grim Reapers, a Louisville bunch. They're riding without their colors, their jackets, because the law has been bearing down on them. That puts them in a bad mood, and these two were fairly drunk besides."

"I thought most motorcyclists get along. I see them waving to each other on the road."

"The good ones are fine, and most are good these days. But there are still a few bad apples. They were busting my chops about owning a rice rocket." He waved hand at the black Kawasaki Ninja that sat beside the gas pump. "Like the convenience store guy said, the deal is they pick a fight. If they knock me out, they take every cent I have."

"I'm glad I could help."

"If I can ever do you a favor..."

"That's okay."

Hardy hurried off toward the truck and yacht. But as he got closer to where the truck had been, he saw it was gone. He looked toward the ramp to the highway, and there it went slowly up and away. In a few seconds, it was out of sight.

Chapter 10

"Sometimes, the thing you are pushing away starts to appear more attractive as it is disappearing into the distance."

HARDY RAN AS FAST AS he could, but there was no way he could catch up to the truck on foot.

He stopped and stood still, staring. *Gone.* They were gone. His insides felt as hollow as a drum. His trip, his adventure, was over, and he was stuck where he stood. All his stuff, what little there was, was gone. Most of all, Ivy and Frosty were off without him too. He wanted to scream or maybe even cry.

At a sound behind him, he spun and saw the black Kawasaki heading toward the same exit the truck had taken. He raced toward it, frantically waving his arms back and forth over his head.

The motorcycle slowed and came over to him. Max lifted the helmet's visor. "What's up, dude?"

"I was stowed away on a yacht that was going across the country."

"Cool."

"Not cool, because it just drove away. Now I can never..."

"Hop on."

Hardy didn't hesitate, nor did he ask if Max was heading that direction anyway. Now was not the time for discussion or to worry that he didn't have a helmet. All he knew was that he wanted to catch up with that yacht.

He hung onto Max as the motorcycle took off like the rice rocket it was.

They shot up the ramp and onto the highway, whizzing past cars and trucks as Max wove back and forth through the lanes. The wind tugged at Hardy. He glanced ahead only once or twice, quickly becoming aware of why motorcyclists wear goggles or helmets, when the rush of wind slammed his eyes shut.

He couldn't see the bike's speedometer, but they made some cars seem to be standing still as they shot out and around them.

Hardy had all he could do to hang on and not go flipping off in the sharp side-to-side swaying as the bike showed all its muscle. The noise seemed deafening. Faces inside windshields and passenger windows turned to see what maniacs were flying along at such a rate of speed.

He had never ridden on a motorcycle before and certainly not one going this fast. It would be a heck of a thing if they skidded off sideways in one of the sharp zigs and zags. He soon figured out the leaning into curves by hanging onto Max's back and following his lean each time.

Every once in a while, he tried to look around and see ahead. The wind rushing at him made that nearly impossible. After a few miles, he finally caught a quick glimpse of the back of the yacht up ahead.

"That's it!" he yelled, not sure if Max had even heard him.

They grew gradually closer. Hardy could make out every detail of the *Pequod II*. That was it, all right. The motorcycle was slowing to keep pace with the traffic around them. Hardy wanted to glance back to see if a state trooper was flashing his lights behind them.

Max turned his head enough to yell back, "Get ready!"

"What?"

Hardy had supposed Max would just follow the truck and let him off when it stopped. He had seconds to realize how wrong he had been.

The bike gave a surge and moved up to the back rear corner of the truck. Hardy had no time to debate what Max intended or to wonder if the driver might glance into his side mirror and see them.

The edge of the truck loomed and grew as close as it could get. Hardy let go of Max and grabbed onto a crossbar that latched the tailgate of the truck. He was immediately yanked off the back of the bike. His feet swung out for a second then went forward to help him grasp the back of the truck. He scrambled up inside as fast as he could go.

The whole thing had taken fractions of a second. His heart was pounding as fast as it could go. He glanced back and doubted if the nearest car, a quarter of a mile back, had seen anything or wondered if it was real if they had. Max moved the motorcycle behind the truck for a moment, gave Hardy a thumbs up, then zoomed on around and out of sight.

Hardy eased down for a moment, panting. He sure wished he had spoken more clearly to Max about what he intended. But here he was!

When traffic was clear behind the truck for a stretch, he climbed up the back of the yacht, went across the deck, and checked the hatch. It was locked. *Good.* He took out his key and opened it.

As soon as he started down the stairs, Frosty came rushing at him, growling. But the growl stopped and shifted to a happy whine, the dog's tail going back and forth as fast as it could.

Frosty jumped up onto Hardy, licking, whining, and wagging his tail.

Ivy came across the cabin toward him. She must have been sprawled on the bed. Her eyes were wet and puffy, but they opened wide when she realized it was him.

She ran across the room and brushed Frosty to one side and grabbed Hardy, squeezing him tightly. "I thought... I thought... I feared you were..."

She was gently sobbing, and he could feel her soft round cheek wet against his neck.

"I'm here again and glad to be back. Do I have permission to come aboard?"

She pulled her head back from his for a second and looked hard at him, taking in every detail of his face. The next thing he knew, her face was pressed against his, and she was kissing him with a happy, eager tongue, and he was kissing her back. His eyes closed, and he brushed at the side of her face, wiping away tears.

Frosty tried to wriggle in between them, but they both gently pushed him to one side. The welcome-back kiss seemed to go on for an hour. Hardy forced himself to pull back from her, to hold her at arm's length and look at her. His knees felt wobbly, and he doubted that was just from jumping through space to grab at the truck.

He said, "Well, I didn't expect that."

"The hell you didn't." Her eyes sparkled, and she couldn't stop grinning. She pulled him close again and hugged him tightly. "I'm glad you made it back."

He could swear that a bolt of electricity had rippled through him with that first kiss.

"Oh, I've got something for you." She took his hand and started to lead him across the cabin.

He had been dreading, expecting this. Well, he didn't feel as much like avoiding it as he had. He was certainly following her along with little resistance.

She stopped at the small breakfast nook by the galley, with its padded seat along the wall and small table bolted to the floor. A white plastic bag sat on the surface. From it she slid a box. As soon as she flipped the lid back, the aroma of barbeque filled the cabin. "It's what I picked up at the stop. There was a small mom-and-pop stand at the back with local foods. You've been saying how you would like to taste the country we're going through as well as see it."

He stood for a moment, knowing his mouth was open. He forced himself to close it. "That's... that's great."

Her eyes narrowed, then they opened wide as she laughed. "Oh. You thought I was tugging you toward the bed, didn't you?"

"I... I..."

She gave his shoulder a push, still chuckling. "Relax. If it comes to that, it will when the time's right. You're hungry. Let's deal with that. It quit being warm a while ago, but it should still taste good."

Frosty was trying to get up on the table.

Ivy pushed him gently back to the floor. "You'll get your turn."

Hardy sat down beside her and let her hand him a napkin then a pork rib dripping in barbeque sauce. The meat was moist and richly flavored. The sauce added just the right tang. Whoever had made the ribs sure knew what they were doing. He soon had a bone picked clean and handed it down to Frosty, who grabbed it from his fingers and went across the cabin to gnaw on the bone while holding it in both paws.

Ivy turned to him. She was still working delicately on her first rib and had a tiny smear of barbeque sauce at the corner of her mouth.

"Well, look at you," he said, "eating something other than cottage cheese or healthy foods."

"I have an appetite too. You should see me around seafood when I get the chance and it's really fresh and good. I'm just usually careful."

His eyes were fixed on her mouth as she spoke.

"I was so worried when we pulled out and you weren't back. I even searched the boat, looked under the Zodiac and everywhere, hoping you were aboard and maybe playing a prank."

"I'm sorry you were upset. I wouldn't prank you, or at least I think I wouldn't. But everything's okay now." He reached for another rib.

Frosty had finished with his first bone and watched Hardy's hands.

"What happened back there?" she asked.

"Oh, a couple of biker-type gangbangers wanted to give a good-citizen biker, Max, a hard time, probably so they could shake him by the ankles until all his money fell out of his pockets."

"And?" The rib she held wasn't all the way picked clean, but she gave it to Frosty and reached for another rib.

"Max didn't want them to do that, nor did I. I thought they should just leave. So we discussed it."

"How'd that come out?"

He finished chewing the bite in his mouth. "Okay. We met in the middle, and they did it my way."

"You must be quite the diplomat."

"I'm just lucky more help came along."

"It was silly of you to step in like that. Brave, but silly too. Mostly silly."

"I think it's the people who stand by and do nothing who do the most harm."

"Does that include me?"

"No. I asked you to get back to the truck. It all turned out well."

"Except for how you got back onto the yacht. How did you?"

"I took a leap of faith." He didn't dare tell her about that, for that truly had been silly. He was just lucky he wasn't lying splattered back there all over the highway.

"I didn't think you'd ever catch up with us again, and then *poof*, you're here. I just hope you didn't take any wild risks."

"None to speak of," he said. "But you're glad I'm back?"

"Very." She snuggled closer to him on the seat.

Chapter 11

As the rest of the day went by, Hardy and Ivy returned to looking out the portholes, calling each other from one side to the other to share the things worth seeing.

Whether it was from his morning activities or just getting back to the yacht and Ivy, Hardy couldn't tell, but he seemed to enjoy each new sight and flavor of the countryside. They were also starting to compare and contrast the different jigsaw pieces of America they'd seen so far.

"The mountains in West Virginia were much bigger than I expected," Ivy said. "The biggest so far."

"I'm starting to realize Kentucky is far more than horse farms and pastures."

But the people going past on the road beside them were as much of the viewing fun.

"These two are a couple, but they've had a tiff. If she presses any harder on that passenger door she's going to pop out, and he's staring straight ahead, hands at ten and two," she said. "Let's hope they relax in a mile or two and remember why they are going somewhere together."

"Here's another load of little-screen people." Hardy pointed toward a loaded SUV going past. Everyone but the driver was staring into a cell phone in one hand.

"That's kind of a pet peeve of yours, isn't it?"

"I don't know. It's really none of my business. I can't tell them how to live their lives. But it makes me sad, all this real world going by, and they're stuck inside that tiny screen world. I'm rarely depressed, lonely, or sad. But they do make me a little sad."

After what seemed an especially busy day, the afternoon stretched out into one languorous scene after another porthole scene until they were watching the sky ahead of the truck shift into bands of pink, purple, and orange as the sun settled across the horizon.

The driver chose that moment to pull into a roadside rest and nestle his cab and trailer behind the big square back of an eighteen-wheeler semi rig.

These were ideal stops since they could watch the driver come and go to the restroom and then know when he had settled down enough for them to make their trips and walk Frosty.

Hardy didn't think it was possible in such a short time, but he saw less of Frosty's ribs. He could ascribe only a little to the meals and the rest to being fluffed up from his bath. The old dog sure looked happier, his tail wagging steadily on every outing.

The cabin grew dimmer until it was hard to see from one end of the cabin to the other.

When it came time for bed, Hardy wasn't sure what to say or do. He decided to do nothing. He got his blanket and book and light out of the cabinet. He settled on the floor, where he had been sleeping. Frosty came over to nestle against him.

Ivy stirred on the bed. "If you're going to read, can you read to me?"

"Sure." He sprang up pretty quickly for someone who should have been tired from his antics of the day.

Ivy scooted all the way to one side of the bed. Before Hardy could get nervous or develop any fancy ideas, Frosty jumped up onto the bed and stretched out next to Ivy. There was just room for Hardy to squeeze onto the other side of the bed.

"There we go," she said. "We're like one happy little family."

Hardy turned on his light and flipped through the pages, deciding to stay with the early going, though he would skip the seasickness part.

"Can I ask you something?" she asked before he could start.

"It's going to be about the book, isn't it?"

"Of course it's about the book. Why one book? Why that one?"

"Well, I have one firm dream, and that's to go to sea on a boat. Until I get to do that, the book takes me out to where I taste salt in the breeze and hear the sharp snap of the canvas as the sails fill with air."

"Oh, just that?"

He had to chuckle that time. The way he'd put it did make him seem almost as possessed or obsessed as Captain Ahab. "I do have a dream of sorts."

"Do tell." Her face this close was everything he could want. He had thought her not pretty once, but there wasn't anything he would change. It was the sort of face he could look at for a very long time.

"One day, I would like to have a small library of my own, with lots of books, all of Twain, Steinbeck, Herodotus, *Arabian Nights*, *The Travels of Marco Polo*, and all my favorite books."

"No Mailer or Vidal?"

"No peacocks allowed. Just real writers."

"I agree. And look at you, thinking about more than one book."

"I guess we're both full of surprises."

"So, you hate writers like Mailer."

"No, not hate. Just because I don't like a thing doesn't mean I hate it. The world doesn't have to be comprised of harsh opposites, just people with different opinions. They can still respect each other, liking different things and living different ways but still getting along."

"Like those schoolmates of yours back on that basketball court?"

"They brought any active dislike to the situation. 'Hey, man, your grades are busting the curve.' Yet they could have studied more and harder, too, and they would have been surfing the curve just fine and not being mad at me for not letting them slack their way through the college coursework. And I would have been just fine being their friend instead of having to defend myself."

"So you're more of a lover than a fighter?"

"I guess you could maybe say that, but not a lover in the way I'm starting to think our truck driver is."

"Ah, so you're monogamous. Very interesting."

"I thought we were talking about books."

"You'd keep Dana, too, in that library of yours?"

"Well, of course I'd keep Dana."

Later that night, he and Frosty lay on the floor once more in the dark, waiting to fall asleep. He thought he had been making a case with Ivy about the world not needing to be so divisive and scrappy about it. But she seemed to be getting way more out of their chat than that. He would have had a hard time making the same intellectual argument with those biker dudes.

He played that whole scene back through his head again and again. Then he started chuckling quietly to himself. He had certainly had a day of it. His heart had been in his throat a couple of times, but in reflection, he was okay with that. He had wanted adventure, and he had sure gotten a dose of that today.

Perhaps his heart was beating faster from the day, or it could have been the gentle snoring and faintly dog-food breath of Frosty, but he didn't doze right off.

The same old insecurities niggled too. Ivy came from a family of old money. He had no real idea of family himself. There had been the other kids, not many of whom got adopted. He'd always thought of himself as naïve when it came to social issues, fast to learn from books, slow to pick up on the nuances of interaction.

Even back then, though, he had figured out the Sandersons got some kind of stipend for each of the youngsters, and there was no encouragement for them to get them adopted. Only an occasional one or two left, and they had been problem kids the Sandersons had probably been glad to see go.

One night, he had sneaked into the Sandersons' office and looked into the file cabinet until he found a file with his name on it. Though they'd always told him his parents had died, he found names and an address.

Later, when he'd briefly had a car, before that messy business of how it ended with Claire, he'd driven to Hartford to see if he could catch a glimpse of his parents. After sitting in the car for the better part of a morning, he did get to see them, except the two people whose names he had read in the file were black.

There must have been some financial advantage to the Sandersons running a farce with wherever the money came from. That made him some kind of "paper orphan" and one who wasn't even sure if his last name was real.

While he was in Hartford, he did get to see Mark Twain's home there. But for the life of him, he couldn't figure how people like the Sandersons could be so cruel as to lie to children about something as important as parents, their name, their family, and even their very identity.

Many of the older kids turned into bullies, the worst of them a big-boned, hulking girl named Maggie, who the others often called Muggie for her tendency to take their lunch money or anything of theirs she might desire. Hardy rarely had money, so she had settled for swinging him around by the ankles and banging him into trees. "Everyone has to have a hobby," she often said.

Maybe something good came of that. It was what led him to a job at the gym so he could get enough training to defend himself.

Otto Rumfeld was the closest thing Hardy ever had to a father figure. Short, squat, and muscular, with a sailor's bowed legs, he walked like some sort of simian, more chimp or orangutan than great ape, though with the great strength of an ape. With two cauliflower ears and a long history of martial arts training in the Navy, he had agreed to give Hardy lessons.

A fellow gym rat named Steve warned Hardy to never go drinking with Otto. He'd been at an Irish bar, sitting on a stool with a pint in front of him, when Otto came up to Steve and said, "Is this guy with you?" He waved a thumb at the guy on the next stool. Otto grabbed the guy and threw him over a group of people onto the jukebox against the wall. The jukebox skipped a beat in the song, and the guy slid to the floor. When the guy managed to stand and look around, no doubt wondering what the hell had happened, he spotted Otto and decided to quietly leave the pub and give up his seat. The bartender didn't kick up a fuss either, having perhaps caught a glimpse or two of the Otto Rumfeld show before.

But Otto had always been kind and instructive to Hardy, and he never drank at work.

On the very first time he was showing Hardy around the gym, Otto waved an expansive arm around the free weights room, exercise machines, and the matted room where aerobics and martial arts training occurred. "This is a busy and complex place, my laddie, and you'll have to be on your toes all the time, eyes open and alert. You get me?"

As he said it, he pushed the door open to the women's locker room and went inside. In seconds, he came popping back out. "And another thing," he said, "don't ever do that."

Otto encouraged Hardy, and when he couldn't afford a better salary, he let Hardy stay in what had been a storage room at the gym. When Hardy landed the job cleaning Mr. Palmer's yacht, Otto didn't mind either. "If you can handle your schoolwork and two jobs, power to you."

Hardy got stable enough to even attract the likes of Claire, but that was another whole train of thought. If he headed down those rails, he never would get to sleep.

His thoughts began to swirl around and around, as they will in the land of half sleep, until they were a blur of bits and pieces of personal history he sought to push away rather than dwell upon.

He concentrated instead on Frosty's steady, almost soothing snore and the sounds of other truck engines idling as their drivers slept. Soon, he was no longer wading through the dregs of his past but had joined all the other sleepers.

Chapter 12

"*By law, a whale is the only animal you're allowed to hunt from a moving vehicle in Tennessee.*"

"*I'll bet whoever made that law didn't expect a boat to be coming through,*" Ivy said.

THE SUN EASED OUT FROM behind a cloud and washed the crowded parking lot with warm sunlight. Nashville was out of sight on the far side of the bypass. They had seen just tips of buildings. But some trucker had his radio on, loud, and the voice was twanging away about trains, trucks, and cheating wives.

Hardy stood on the yacht's deck, trying to calm Frosty. "Don't worry, old fellow. She'll be back. Just you wait."

The air was filled with the steady hum of vehicles on the nearby highway, the sound of trucks slowing or taking off again, their loud air brakes *bracka-bracka-bracki*ng, and yells back and forth from some of the truckers in the parking lot as they headed to climb back into their rigs. Hardy suspected that most of them probably still used CB radios in addition to staying in touch with cell phones. Guys could poke fun at women for talking a lot, but take a group of men at a sports bar or at a construction site or in a group of truckers getting together, and they could outtalk any clutch of females.

These men weren't lightweights either, for the most part. The combination of sitting all day and eating high-carb meals was taking its toll. One guy going across the lot in large, loose pants looked like a one-man sack race. Others had the acquired swagger that a big belly gave them. At least the guy driving their truck was reasonably fit—well, at least compared to many of the drivers Hardy had seen.

A big group of truckers had gathered to crowd inside the stop's restaurant. He had been hoping the service inside would be slow for their truck's driver, to buy them a little time. But no, that was him coming this way. Hardy could clearly see the blue shirt but saw no sign of Ivy. Then he spotted her, trailing in the distance, carrying a bag and slipping behind one parked truck to the next though the driver wasn't looking back.

Hardy took Frosty below and locked the hatch.

He waited until he heard the driver climb up onto the deck, check the hatch, and have his usual look around. As the driver climbed back down, Hardy unlocked the hatch.

The truck's engine started. Frosty started to whine and go back and forth below the stairs.

"She's coming," Hardy said.

Seconds later, steps hurried across the deck, and the hatch opened. Ivy came bustling down into the cabin and had to endure a tail-wagging frenzy of nudging and nuzzling from Frosty.

The truck started to move.

"At least I didn't have to jump through the air to get onto the truck's moving back end."

"Oh. You figured that out?"

She gave his shoulder a shove. "Of course I did. Not all of the details, which I'm not sure I want to know, but please don't ever do that again... unless you have to."

"I recall a time when *you* barely made it back on."

"And I needed a hand. Yeah. Yeah."

She carried her packages over to the breakfast nook table.

"You sure bought a lot." Hardy felt his usual ongoing twinge of guilt about not carrying his end of the food purchases.

"Not to worry. You're the one who secured us the ride."

"Kind of."

"Look what I got us." She dug into one of the bags she had carried. From it she took a black cloth square, which she unfolded into a foot-by-foot-and-a-half flag. The black flag was centered with the usual white skull and crossbones. The lettering above and below the symbol said, "The beatings will continue... until morale improves."

"Now we have a pirate flag if we need one at any point," she said.

"But we don't have a mast to run it up."

She chuckled to herself.

"What?" he asked.

She shook her head, still giggling.

He didn't push at her private joke. She was enjoying herself far too much and needed no help from him. "What smells so good?"

"I managed to pick up some local flavor. There was a food truck in the parking lot with genuine smells coming from it." She slid the boxes out of the bags. "Here you have your fried pickles, some catfish, and, of course, cornbread."

Hardy had to put a hand out to keep Frosty from climbing up onto the small table. "I guess catfish is a kind of seafood for you, isn't it?"

"It'll do until we get near an ocean again."

BECAUSE THE DAY WAS bright and their stomachs were full, Tennessee provided some of the best and most enjoyable viewing so far. The green hills rolled up and out of sight to the horizon, the farm houses and silos popped into view like mushrooms, and everywhere they looked across the countryside, they could see something new and fresh that had them calling back and forth to each other from their porthole views.

Hardy knew there were deep lakes just out of sight, home to some of the largest smallmouth bass in the country. He would've liked to see the boats out on them, fishing. But the truck kept to the highway, rolling purposefully along on its mission.

The driver made only one quick diversion by pulling into a rest stop. But he was all too soon heading back to the truck at a hurried pace. Hardy, who had slipped around behind the building to use the bushes so that the driver wouldn't see him, had to scramble to get to the truck as it was starting.

They hadn't been spotted by the truck's driver because they were getting quite good and clever about knowing where the truck's blind spots were, where they could hide when getting on each time. Hardy also kept his distance from the driver whenever possible so that he didn't wake up to the notion that he was seeing the same people at each stop. From the way she approached the truck each time, he could tell Ivy was doing the same.

On the way up the ladder, he realized that he was looking forward to being with Ivy and Frosty again, that he was missing them, and that they were becoming a part of him. It didn't seem that very long ago that he'd been avoiding her.

As he went down into the cabin, Frosty came rushing to him. Ivy grinned from across the room. No big hug this time, but sometimes a really good grin could feel like a hug.

By the afternoon, they were watching portions of the city of Memphis roll past like a steamboat. Oh, how he wished they could stop and see Beale Street, Graceland, and the Blues Hall of Fame or eat some of the local barbeque or fried chicken. Even without a radio on, he was hearing the sounds of Elvis Presley, B.B. King, and Johnny Cash.

If there was a downside to traveling this way, it was not getting to stop, walk the streets, explore the parks, smell the scents, and hear the sounds of the many places they passed. But even so, this was like a sampler run, a slice through the country to show him all he ought to experience more fully someday, and there sure was a lot of that.

They didn't get the chance to see or experience people much either, except the occasional convenience store clerk. It would be nice to have conversations, to get a feel for what each region's people felt, what they valued, and what they wanted in life. He'd always felt that once he knew what someone wanted, he knew a lot more about the person.

Then they were crossing the wide, wide Mississippi River, one of the grandest iconic sights in America, drawing its water from miles of land to its north as it flowed south from its headwaters in Minnesota down toward New Orleans. He knew why Twain had fallen in love with the river, on a steamboat watching for sandbars and snags in a job most young boys dreamed of then.

He rushed from his porthole to the one on the other side to soak in as much as possible of the view of all that muddy water heading down through the middle of the nation, his imagination going wild with the adventures to be had up and down that length. Another whole story could happen there, one he ached to experience one day.

Arkansas looked different to Hardy as soon as they started through it, not rough and brutish, but still a little wild and untamed. He suspected, from a couple of trucks that went by, that some of the local people liked it that way. He saw some rebel-flag bumper stickers and one gun rack in the back window of a truck though there was no gun in it. Another pickup was piled high with household goods as someone made a move. A rolled-up rug and a wooden rocking chair at the top of the pile on its side made him think of *The Beverly Hillbillies*. But he stopped himself from where he was going with that biased thought.

He was in no position to understand the lives of others at a glance, or worse, to judge. Compared to what was in his wallet right now, that family crowded into that crew-cab truck had more of a right to look down on him than the other way around. The thought took him back to thinking about the social distance and difference between himself and Ivy again instead of just savoring the time they were sharing together. He shook it off as best he could.

Ivy sat beside him with Frosty across her lap. She stroked the dog's head and back as she smiled out the window.

"It's a wonder other folks don't try to climb on this boat and ride for a spell," she said.

"One did back at that truck stop on the outskirts of Nashville," Hardy said. "But I was on the deck. I just stood and wagged a finger from side to side, and he turned his face so I couldn't see it and slinked back from the direction he came—made me feel like one of those railroad bulls with a railroad-switch club in hand as he rousted hobos off the train as they tried to climb into an open boxcar."

After traveling along a short stretch of highway through the state, the driver pulled off at a ramp where there was no rest stop or truck stop. The truck stayed on the access road until it could cross over to the other side beneath an overpass.

The driver went back on a two-lane road a short ways then jockeyed the truck around until he could park it beside a trailer court on one side and an expanse of open field and woods on the other side of the road.

"I think we're doing pretty well for having no sense of this driver's pattern," Ivy said. "He knows the rest stops and truck stops, but we don't, nor do we know how long he'll stay in each. He stops. He goes. It all seems as much by whim as anything."

"We've been lucky so far," Hardy said. "Shhh." He held a finger to his lips.

Ivy held Frosty's muzzle and kept his growl low as the driver checked the hatch and found it locked. He climbed back down off the back of the yacht and truck.

"Oh, my," she said. "This is the closest we've been to a chance to walk through woods and feel nature."

Hardy was watching the driver walking through the trailers. He didn't see a woman coming to greet the driver this time, but he guessed that was probably the reason for the unusual stop.

"Do you think our driver is something of a playboy?" Ivy asked.

"He's a good and careful driver, even a slow one, which is okay with me. But in a couple of spots, he seems to pick up his pace on land and become a real Lothario," Hardy agreed. "Some of that's conjecture based on just a couple of instances, but I suspect it's a pretty sound guess."

"I think twice in one trip with different women makes a statement of sorts." Ivy's lips had pulled tight into a disapproving pout.

"We haven't seen this woman," Hardy said. "And one might even be his wife. But I have to agree with you. I wouldn't call him faithful or monogamous."

"I wonder how he met them all."

Hardy could have disputed that two women hardly amounted to "them all." He could see she was warming up on the subject, which made him anxious to change it. "We can at least take advantage of his dalliance, or whatever, and move around some."

The first thing they did was to take Frosty for a walk. Hardy fastened his makeshift leash, and Ivy handed the dog down to him. He gave her the end of the leash, and they crossed the road and started off through the open field. That side of the road was open and undeveloped and untamed. The grass and sprinkling of wildflowers came up to their shins. In the other direction, on the far side of the trailer court, he could see a convenience store a block or so away.

When they got to the far side of the patch of prairie, a wide spot of bare dirt marked the opening of an often-traveled path into the shadows of the woods generated by a thick canopy of tree limbs that met and interlaced above their heads.

He took a deep breath and caught the scent of earth, a rich loamy soil accompanied by the smell of green and growing plants. It was a wonderful smell, right up there with the salty and sometimes fishy smell of the sea. These were the aromas that made him feel alive and appreciate being so.

The moment was made richer by having Ivy and Frosty along, sharing the sights, sounds, and smells. Ivy grinned back at him, and Frosty sniffed away, at a plant one second and at a toad in the shadow of a leaf the next.

Birds chirped and called out in the distance. A lizard scuttled off to slip under the overhang of a rounded limestone rock. Leaves rustled above them as a breeze combed the tops of the trees.

Frosty was long enough in the tooth to walk well on leash, not to pull but to keep pace with Ivy, pausing often to sniff at bushes, rocks, and tufts of grass.

The canopy of leaves and limbs meeting above them made the trail cool, and a breeze that rustled the trees added to that.

"We should do this sort of thing more often," Ivy said.

"You know why we don't. We don't know the pattern of our driver well enough to count on chances to get out like this."

The sides of the trail had grown up with occasional wildflowers, mossy fallen logs, and here and there a sprinkle of poison ivy that they avoided.

A patch of blackberry plants on one slope soon grew into a bigger tangle, full of spiders and sweet berries. Around a bend in the path, they came upon a dogwood tree in full bloom. Patches of bluestem bunchgrass formed fluffy mounds on the hillsides that sloped up into the thicker stands of trees on either side.

Hardy couldn't ask for a more refreshing pause in their roll across America. Some of his favorite times growing up, when he hadn't been really wicked by sneaking off to the library, were walks outdoors, and especially in the woods. The crunch of the trail beneath their steps and each new thing that attracted Frosty's sniffing nose pleased him as well. The air seemed richer, fresher, and it relaxed him to his core.

One tree had a waterline mark a foot up from its base.

Hardy chuckled to himself. "The only story I know about Arkansas is about a farmer who wanted to sell his land along the Mississippi

River. A potential buyer was touring the land but saw watermarks five and six feet up the trunks of the trees. 'Does this land flood much?' he asked. 'Naw. Them marks are from the hogs a-rubbin' their backs.' When they finished the tour, the farmer asked if the guy was willing to buy the property. The guy said, 'Naw. But I wouldn't mind havin' a start on some of them hogs.'"

"Oh my gosh," Ivy said. "You have a sense of humor. Not razor-edged. But it's there. We could be in a sitcom."

"In a sitcom, the lives of the characters are filled with one tiny crisis after another until one big crisis barely solved renders the others moot. And each crisis is almost always caused by some miscommunication or other."

"That could be us. We could do that."

He grinned and nodded. "I guess we could." The wind coming through the trees pressed against his face and smelled cool and fresh and a little damp, the kind in which fungi could readily grow. Not a bad thing, he thought.

They kept walking, though he slowed. They didn't dare wander too far. He turned and started back.

"You can learn a lot in a walk through a woods," he said.

"Like what?"

"Like a butterfly will just as soon land on a weed or dog poop as on a flower."

"I suppose that's pretty handy to know." She gave him a head tilt and then shook her head at his brand of a philosophical moment.

Chapter 13

Soon, Hardy and Ivy worked their way back along the trail until they could see the truck.

"What do you think our driver is up to?" Ivy asked.

"I think we can agree on the what. It's the who that's a puzzle. My theory is that he has more than one woman along his regular path that he stops to visit."

"I'm betting they all make him pie, too, or homemade dumplings," Ivy said. "Because he's fit but not what I'd call slim."

"Or particularly attractive," Hardy said. "But he must have the patter for love."

Ivy tilted her head at him but said nothing.

When they had Frosty back in the cabin and had fed and watered him, they climbed back down and hiked to the convenience store, dumping their usual small trash sack into the container outside the front door.

Before they went in, Ivy said, "Don't worry about money. I know you probably didn't carry along much. I've got credit cards that will get us through. We'll let the plastic do the talking."

Hardy didn't know how he felt about that. Embarrassed? But there was no other choice. He suspected that if he opened his wallet, moths would fly out.

"Besides, my father texted me that he wasn't able to pay you for your last cleaning of the boat. He couldn't find you anywhere." She chuckled. "So you have that coming, and since I'm spending my father's money..."

He didn't know how he felt about that either. It still seemed a lot like freeloading, but he guessed so was stowing away on the yacht and getting a free ride. This probably wasn't a good time to get into a moral debate with himself.

"Are you still getting text messages?" he asked.

"Nope. My phone needs charging. We'll have to wait on the next opportunity to do that."

They took turns in the men's and women's bathrooms, where there was no chance for a shower. Then they got water, some breakfast bars for the morning, and some ready-made turkey-and-tomato-on-rye sandwiches. Hardy checked but wasn't able to find cottage cheese in the limited dairy section. But the store had damn all in the way of every kind of chip, potato or corn, and had stacks of canned sodas on every endcap display.

Dark was settling in as they got back to the truck and climbed up onto the boat's deck.

In the dark shadows growing beneath bushes and some tall grass, a lightning bug blinked on then off. Another, farther away, flicked on then off.

"Oh, let's watch those," he said.

Her eyes opened wide. "Sure, if that gives you joy."

"It does."

They stowed their purchases below and went back onto the deck with their sandwiches.

"I'm sorry I couldn't get something tastier to represent the local cuisine," Ivy said. "That *is* one of the joys of travel, sampling the flavors as well as the views of an area."

"That's okay. The walk, the scenery, and the company more than make up for that."

She grinned out at the spectacle of the early blinking lights in the growing dark.

Frosty ended up getting a piece of one of Hardy's sandwiches and an even bigger chunk from Ivy. He curled up at their feet as more and more lightning bugs began to flicker in the dark. They moved about, gradually getting higher in whatever mating ritual they were observing.

"In an old copy of a *Pogo* book, I recall him asking a lightning bug why he turned on his light at night. The bug said, 'To attract females.' Pogo asked, 'Then why do you turn it off?' The bug said, 'To sneak up on them.'"

"I can't fault the range of books you have read and apparently learned from." She chuckled.

"This is one of my favorite times of the year." Hardy took a deep breath of night air. "It's always a treat to watch them."

"Do you like driving through the countryside in the fall when all the leaves are turning colors and the woods are mottled with yellow, red, and orange?"

"Of course. But if I had to pick a favorite season, it would be spring."

"Because everything is turning a light green after all the snow and cold?"

"And also because that's when I can go into the woods and hunt for spring mushrooms, morels."

"Do you eat them?"

"Lightly battered and fried in butter, few things are better than morels."

"Most anything would be better cooked that way—an old shoe, for instance."

"I also like the time of year when Vidalia onions come onto the market or Rome apples."

"Are a lot of your favorite things about food?"

"I guess. I've been hungry before. It makes me appreciate some things more."

They sat in silence, watching the lightning bugs get higher and higher until they were in the upper limbs of the distant trees, giving them an almost Christmaslike flickering.

"You ever hurt anyone with that jiu jitsu stuff?" she asked.

"I try not to. That's not the point."

"I'll bet you're one of those guys who goes through life thinking everyone is just waiting to pick on you. You've prepared for just that, haven't you?"

In his orphanage days, he had heard Mr. Sanderson call his wife Fran, and she called him Burt. But the children were only allowed to call them Mr. or Mrs. Sanderson. The Sandersons' house-discipline rule was to let the kids sort themselves out, which led to a tyranny of bigger over smaller, and Hardy had always been one of the smaller boys. He had developed a lifelong dislike of bullies, and that was what had led to his self-defense training and eventual teaching.

When he didn't answer, she asked, "What *is* the point?"

He looked her in the eyes. "To not be the person getting hurt myself. Me and anyone I care for."

"Now it's getting interesting," she said. "Have you ever cared for anyone before?"

He still wasn't ready to talk about Claire.

"I'm keeping the car," Claire had told him. "You put it in my name. Remember?"

Hardy had handed her the bank payment book. "Don't miss a payment," he said.

"You're not going to pay for it?"

He hadn't needed to answer that and had turned and walked away.

"Once or twice," he said to Ivy.

"Didn't go well?"

"Not very."

The sky around them was about as dark as it could get. The lightning bugs had mostly lifted up and out of sight, except for one or two stragglers who now looked lonely as they blinked on and off near the ground.

The wind rustled the grass and the tops of the distant trees.

"If you were ever going to be in a relationship again, what would you be looking for?" Her voice sounded pensive, a little uncertain.

He shook his head. Here he was in his adventure of a tour across America, and he was suddenly in a conversation about relationships. Maybe the driver's actions had brought that on.

He thought for a moment of the things he didn't want: selfish, vengeful, or overbearing. But he said, "What I would most want are: loyalty, faithfulness, a sense of humor, passion, shared interests in common, and an ongoing and restless curiosity over intelligence."

"You don't want intelligence?"

"I didn't say that. What I—"

"You said earlier that you don't get lonely or depressed. Does that mean you prefer solitude?"

"I've been alone a lot in my life."

"That doesn't mean you need to keep being alone the rest of your life."

"I guess I've prepared myself for that contingency, though."

She didn't respond right away, which was fine with him. They had been steadily easing away from his comfort zone, and he was beginning to experience a restless thin-ice feeling.

"You think you've become a little antisocial?" she asked.

"It's okay. I'm working on it."

"You're working on it by going off on your own like this?"

"I'm not on my own now," he said.

"But that wasn't your choice."

"It's not a perfect plan."

"What was your major in college?" she asked.

"I had two majors: communications and business."

"So why aren't you a better communicator?"

"I'm trying," he said. *It was such a great day, until now.*

There he had been, trying to relax and talk idly about nothing, and the conversation had slipped away and turned on him. She had steered it to get more out of it than he had expected to share.

She stood and moved over until she was by the hatch, ready to go below. He couldn't tell if her shoulders were shaking. He got up, and Frosty followed. They went over to her. He was trying hard to think through everything he'd said.

"Can we just...?" He stopped speaking and listened, turning to look hard into the dark around them.

She started to say something.

He reached and put a hand over her mouth. "Shh." He pointed.

She moved his hand away from her mouth and peered into the night. "But—"

"Shh," he whispered again, as close to her ear as he could get.

In the shadows, something almost as dark moved. The shape of a person slowly emerged from the direction they'd taken to go to the convenience store. The steps were furtive. It was a man. He glanced all around before he scurried toward the truck.

"That's not our driver," Hardy whispered into her ear.

The door of the cab opened and closed.

"I sure hope our driver hasn't left his keys in the ignition." She squeezed Hardy's arm.

"Or that this guy doesn't know how to hotwire a truck," he said.

Then the truck's engine started.

Chapter 14

"I was just reading where the theft of semitrucks isn't as common as it used to be," Hardy mumbled.

"Tell that to whoever is behind the wheel up there."

"What a time for the driver to leave the keys in the truck," Ivy said as they scrambled down the stairs to the cabin.

"His mind must have been on something else."

"I know what it was on, but that's no excuse."

Hardy hurried over to the cabinet, dug around in his bag, and came back with a pen and a small pad of paper.

"What are you doing?" she asked.

"Writing down the route we take, just in case," he said.

"I don't think I want to know in case of what." She held onto Frosty tightly, with both small fists clutching clumps of black fur. He didn't whimper or cry out, just snuggled closer.

"Help me look out the portholes," Hardy said. "We want every street name or highway number."

"Okay. But I don't know what good it can do."

"Right now, it's about all we can do."

"I wish my blasted phone..."

"Wishing won't help us either."

"Humpf."

She took up a position at a porthole on the far side and quickly took to the task, calling out anything she saw that might act as a trail marker. Along one dark stretch where they rolled along on a two-lane road with nothing especially noteworthy to see, she muttered, "I don't know what good this will do us."

"It's about hope," Hardy said, "and being prepared if we get the least chance."

"I sure wish I could just call the cops."

"I'd probably get arrested too," he said, "along with whoever the hell is driving this truck."

They seemed to be getting farther away from lights and civilization with every mile the truck rolled.

"Hardy?"

"Yeah?"

"Hardy?"

"What?"

"I'm worried. Guys who steal trucks are professionals."

"If you want to draw the fine line, anyone who gets money out of doing something is a professional. A paperboy gets paid, so he's one."

"I mean guys like this are criminal thugs."

"What they amount to are people who can't get and maintain legitimate jobs, so they stoop to risking serious jail time against the few bucks they get for a job like this."

"I'll bet a yacht sells for more than a few bucks."

"You're right there. Our driver seems the sort to usually be careful about such things. Whatever it was, or whoever it was in that trailer court to make him take lively steps getting there, must sure be special to him."

"I'm sure it'll be a mark against him that he lost a whole truck and a boat."

"Can't be a good thing. I was starting to like the guy even though we know very little about him."

"I'm more worried about whoever is driving the truck right now," she said. "I don't think anyone who goes around stealing trucks does so because they are educated and their career is going well."

"That's probably why a lot of guys back in the day went out to sea as pirates. It was the only way left for them, stealing, plundering, and pillaging."

"I hope no plundering or whatever is going to happen," Ivy said.

"I imagine the guy's focus is just on stealing the yacht for now. Getting the truck too is a bonus."

"What can we do?"

"We've got a pirate flag now. Maybe you should run it up, because we're going to have to do something."

"I know where there are some refrigerator magnets. Dad had them for charts and maps, though they were never to be used near the ship's compass."

She probably knew what he was up to, trying to keep her mind from fixating on fear and danger, but all the same, she busied herself putting their small pirate flag on the fridge.

The truck took another right turn onto an even smaller road.

"You'd better get back to your porthole, matey," he said. "There are some new trail markers to keep track of, just in case."

"Aye, or should I say argh."

The truck began to slow.

"Uh oh," she said.

A high metal fence ran alongside the road where they were slowing. They were high enough above it for Hardy to see glimmers of shapes beyond the fence. There were some RVs in one row, along with a couple of trucks, but most of it looked like a junkyard.

Yet coiled razor wire ran across the top of the metal wall of the fence. That wasn't a good sign. Something inside was worth keeping people out, perhaps other stolen vehicles.

The truck went past the lane to the gate then stopped and began to back up into the lane and moving toward the gate.

"We'd better go topside and get ready," Hardy said.

"Ready for what?"

"Anything."

The air was cooler as Hardy stepped out onto the deck. The breeze was still steady and in his face. He didn't see a sign of lightning bugs anywhere around them.

He held onto a gunwale until the truck stopped. The truck's headlights lit up the short lane back to the road, but the stretch behind the tail end of the yacht was dim. Hardy could barely make out that the gate seemed to be closed from the inside.

The truck's engine idled.

The driver came around and went up to a small box with a button. He pressed the button then pressed it again.

A tinny voice came out of the small box by the button. "What?"

"It's Garen. I have a surprise load."

"Okay. I'm coming."

He waited, restlessly shifting his weight from one foot to the other, either nervous or possibly a drug user. He wore jeans, boots, and a dark hoodie, which he tugged back from where it covered his head to let his shaggy, unkempt hair spill out. He had a hungry leanness about him.

Ivy came up close behind Hardy. He pulled her closer and whispered into her ear. "I say we go. Now."

"And do what?"

"If we can just get to the cab before..." He was already scrambling down the yacht's ladder and then the back of the truck.

Ivy's movement coming down the back of the truck made a loud click behind him.

Garen, the guy standing at the gate spun, saw them, and pulled a knife out of his right boot, with a flash of its silver six-inch blade.

The gate was starting to open. Another man stuck his head out then came all the way once he seemed to have an idea of what was going on. He wore jeans but had no shirt on his lean tattooed torso, looking just like almost every perp ever to appear on real-crime television. His dark hair came down to his neck and was matched in color by a scruffy short beard.

"Get in the cab," Hardy hissed to Ivy.

But Ivy stayed. "I want to help."

Garen rushed forward, directly toward Ivy, probably figuring she would be easier to get out of the way.

He gave Ivy's shoulder a shove. "Get going. That's how you can help most."

Hardy stepped into the path of the charging Garen.

Ivy reluctantly spun and took off in a jog.

Hardy stayed focused on Garen, who was rushing toward him.

The other man was reaching for something just inside the gate.

As Garen got close, he raised the knife high in a flash of silver in the dim light. He brought that arm down as he got to Hardy, who stepped forward and curled his left arm around the knife arm while he bent back at his waist, his right leg extending past the running man's right knee.

Hardy snapped forward at his waist, gripping the knife arm tightly and slamming his right hand high on the guy's chest. His right leg snapped back with the motion at the same time and struck the back of Garen's knee, buckling him as the hand to his chest shoved him backward.

Hardy knew he had pulled his punch as soon as the man struck the gravel of the drive. Done correctly, his right arm should have slammed against the man's esophagus, possibly breaking it, and the slam to the ground might well have cracked the skull. The person falling has no way to break the fall. But he hadn't wanted to kill the man, just to disable him until they could get away.

He paid the price for going easy on the guy when the knife turned in Garen's hand and slashed across Hardy's forearm.

Hardy let go, took a quick step back and kicked at the knife hand, sending the knife flying through the air. The guy reached up to grab hold of Hardy's clothes with a tight, desperate grip.

The other man was running toward Hardy as fast as he could go. He waved a piece of pipe high in his right hand. Perhaps it had been leaning just inside the gate for just such a moment as this.

He was almost upon Hardy, who was struggling to get free. The guy swung back the pipe. Something hit him from behind, and his knees buckled.

Hardy brought up a knee that caught the guy holding him in the chin. The clutching fingers let go as Garen slumped back to the ground.

The guy with the pipe was trying to turn to strike at something gripping his jeans and pulling.

Hardy stepped in and grabbed the guy's wrist, twisting the pipe out of his hand. He threw it as far away as he could. When the guy turned toward him, Hardy gave a full kick with his toe landing in the V of the man's legs. He knew a whole lot of fancier things he could have done, but he wanted quick, and that was quick.

As the guy dropped to his knees, clutching at himself, Hardy could see that Frosty had a grip on the man's jeans and was pulling back with all four legs. He'd been the one to slam into the guy from behind and distract him.

A white-hot flash of fire shot through Hardy. The man had been swinging that pipe toward Frosty, hoping to maim or kill him. His anger was so intense that he nearly stepped forward to kick the man again while he was down. But he shook it off at the last second.

"Come on, Frosty!" Hardy ran along the side of the yacht to the passenger side of the cab. He yanked the door open. Frosty came limping toward him. Hardy grabbed the dog and hoisted him up inside the cab, got in himself, and slammed his door shut.

Ivy hit the clutch twice with her left foot as she shifted into first gear. The truck jerked ahead in an eager lurch.

Hardy looked in the side view mirror on his side and saw at least one of the men getting to his feet to start running after them.

But Ivy quickly double-clutched again into second gear and was all the way into third by the time she made her turn as she swung the truck onto the road in a spray of dirt and gravel.

"I didn't know you knew how to drive a double-clutch truck."

She laughed. "Some of the companies Dad owns are shipping ones. He let me have a go at driving an eighteen-wheeler when I was still in my teens. It's something you don't forget."

"I'm glad you didn't."

She looked down at his arm. "Oh my gosh! You're hurt."

"So is Frosty. He was limping on the way to the cab."

"I mean your arm."

He looked down. His arm had a three-inch-long slash across it. Blood was filling the wound and starting to flow out, smearing across his arm. His first thought was to not get blood all over the inside of the cab. He could see a white roll of paper towels just behind Ivy's seat. He grabbed for it and started wrapping thick, tight layers around the wound, trying to close it and apply pressure at the same time.

The blood was seeping through, but he was slowing it. The arm began to throb.

"Oh my gosh. Oh my gosh. We need to do something."

"You're doing it, Ivy. You're driving. Remember our landmarks. I think there's a turn to the left just ahead."

He would have paused to admire the way she downshifted, made the turn, and started working back up to speed again. Her thin, athletic legs seemed barely to reach the pedals, but she was driving the truck as if she knew what she was doing.

Chapter 15

Ivy glanced in her mirrors. "No one's behind us." The road ahead was empty and dark where the headlights couldn't reach.

Hardy hadn't expected the thieves to get in a vehicle and come after them. Their grasping an opportunity to steal had fallen flat. They would probably just wait for another chance. Besides, he hoped he'd hobbled them enough that they needed to tend to their own bruises.

Ivy slowed and stopped in the road. She fished a flashlight out of the glove box and went back into the sleeper area. She dug around and finally emerged with half a roll of duct tape. "Whew," she said. "Kind of gamey back there. No wonder he grabs at any other place to sleep he can."

She turned on the overhead light, pulled a strip of silver tape from the spool, and used her teeth to start a tear. Then she peeled off the blood-soaked paper towels from his arm and threw them out her window.

With both hands, she drew the sides of the wound together then took the strip of tape hanging from her mouth and stretched it across to hold the wound closed. "That will have to do for now." She wrapped more paper towels around the arm, using more tape to hold those in place.

"Keep pressure on it too." She turned back and put the truck in gear, and they were off again.

"Frosty is hurt too," Hardy said. "He was limping."

"He probably just hyperextended a leg from jumping down to the ground from the back of the truck. He'll likely be fine in a day or so. You, we still need to tend to."

"You're pretty handy to have around," he said. "Is your course of study premed? Or at least heading to be a vet so you can help Frosty?"

"I started with premed studies but switched," she said. "Now it's marine biology."

"Oh. Why?"

"So I can figure out fish heads like you."

"I guess I never asked as much about you as I should have."

"We can discuss that later, now that we're communicating." She tried to give him a scowl but broke out laughing instead. She swung her head back to fix on the road ahead. "Now, give me a hand with those trail markers we were keeping track of so we can get this tub back where she belongs."

When the truck was rolling along a longer stretch of the route back, she asked, "How did you come to get hurt? I thought this self-defense stuff was intended to keep that from happening."

"It was my fault. I just wanted to disable them, not kill them."

"I think if someone is trying to kill you, then you might need to rethink your priorities in the moment. This isn't all the kind of stuff that happens on a mat in the gym out here."

"So I am coming to understand." His arm was throbbing in time to the beat of his heart.

"Next time, do what you need to do."

"Since you almost entered the field of medicine, doesn't the Hippocratic Oath say something about first doing no harm?"

"It does."

"That's sort of my watchword too."

"Well, I won't do harm as long as I'm at least the medic on board. But you're free to break other people's bones or whatever you need to do to keep yourself and Frosty and me safer. Fortunately, I think you're fixable, expect for maybe tinkering with the inside of your head."

"My head is fine."

"So you say, but now you're on the injured list."

He had to refer to his written-out trail-marker notes a couple of times, but they eventually pulled into the street where they had been parked. At least no one was standing in the empty spot, waiting for them. She jockeyed the truck around until she had it where it had been parked before.

"That was an amazing bit of driving," Hardy said.

"Will it help if I tell you I was terrified the whole time?"

"But it needed doing, and you did it."

They cleaned the inside of the truck's cab as well as they could, putting everything back where it had been, even leaving the keys in the ignition and the driver's door unlocked the way it had been left in his haste.

"We sure used up a lot of his paper towels," Hardy said.

"I don't think that's the sort of thing guys notice or worry about," Ivy said. "He'll probably be busy kicking himself for leaving his keys in the rig and being thankful no one stole it."

"He did lose a little fuel in the bargain, but that's a small thing."

When Hardy started to climb up the back of the truck, Ivy stepped close to help him.

"I can make it," he said then felt immediately sorry for snapping.

But she must have known he was just irritable because of fretting about his wound, so she stepped back and said nothing. Once he was on the truck, she lifted Frosty up to him. Hardy took most of the weight with his uninjured arm. Ivy climbed up to help him get the dog up the yacht's back ladder as well.

Hardy went over to the breakfast nook table and sat down. The makeshift wrappings on his arm were soaked through with blood, some of it starting to dry brown on the edges. Frosty came over to him and rested his head on Hardy's thigh.

"Dogs know when you're hurt." She got his flashlight out and bustled around, getting a bowl, some of the last of their bottles of water, and towels.

"We could use a sewing kit too," Hardy said.

"What?"

"At least a needle and thread. The sewing stuff on board is for mending sails, pretty big needle and all."

"Oh, you would like that, a big old gnarly scar on your arm like a battle tattoo."

"Argh." His arm had settled into a steady, slow throb now that he was moving around less.

"We have an hour or two before our Prince Charming of a driver stirs and comes back to find he left his keys in the cab." She brought the ship's first aid kit to the table.

"It's kind of lucky he did," Hardy said. "If the thief had hot-wired the truck, we might not have had such an easy time getting it back to where we are."

"Leave it to you to find the silver lining in all this." She set up his flashlight by propping it up to point at the table. She opened the kit and took out a roll of tape, a box of gauze, a tube of Neosporin and a box of Steri-Strips. "I'm the one who stocked the kit, so I knew these were in there." She held up the box of Steri-Strips. "They're as good as butterfly sutures, and that means we won't have to use any needle and thread on you."

"Oh, rats." He moved his arm on the table and winced. He had kind of pictured himself looking away in manly, stoic silence while she sewed the wound shut with a needle and black thread, biting the end of thread off with those white teeth of hers.

"Are you in pain?" she asked.

"A little."

"I've got you some aspirin and ibuprofen. They can help a little, but in the Old West, they would have given you a shot of whiskey to help with our little procedure."

"There's always..."

"I'm way ahead of you." She went over to a lower cabinet, opened the top of a crate, and came back to the table with a bottle of Dom Perignon. Then she got a couple of stemmed glasses from where they'd been strapped in place in a cabinet and brought them to the table.

"I was being careful not to get into that case," Hardy said.

"It's for the greater good." She worked the cork off in the correct fashion so that there wasn't a loud pop and waste of the champagne. She filled the two glasses.

She got out two aspirins and an ibuprofen from the kit and held them up to his mouth, which he opened. She popped them in and handed him his glass. He washed down the pills while she was reaching for her glass.

"I understand me needing a drink, but should you be drinking?" he asked. "Doctor on duty and all?"

"Believe me. I need this as much as you do." She took a sip from her glass. "Mmm."

"This is a helluva time to celebrate," he said.

"I don't know. Maybe it's the most apt time yet. We just accomplished a great feat. Several, in fact. Someone stole the truck, and we got it back before our driver even knew it was gone. And we did it with *almost* no injuries."

He frowned down at his forearm but emptied his glass. She drank the rest of hers and filled the glasses again. "Now, let's do this thing."

At first, he looked away as she peeled back the tape and paper towels with their dried, crusty blood. "I need to clean and disinfect the wound. You'd better keep drinking." She poured him another glass. "Good thing this stuff is cheap."

"Yeah. Right," he said.

"Are you getting any pain relief from the pills too?"

"No. But I'm starting to ride a righteous buzz from the champagne. I'm not much of a drinker, except to celebrate once in a while."

"Whee." She dabbed at the open wound with paper towels she wetted by dipping them into the bowl of water.

Hardy felt sorry for a moment that they were messing up a few of the boat's towels for the chore, since they would be hard to clean even if they could get them to a laundromat.

He continued looking away most of the time, but the glance or two he shot at the wound made him a little woozy, looking in to see the red meat of the inside of his arm.

She put all the bloody wrappings and tape she had peeled away into one of their plastic bags.

When she had the wound as cleaned out as she could get it, she applied the disinfectant along the inside of the wound and especially along the edges. Then she held the wound together with her fingers as she applied each Steri-Strip, keeping them a half inch apart until they formed a row, holding the wound tightly closed. The cut had quit bleeding, except for a tiny drop here and here, which she dabbed at and cleaned away with a wet paper towel.

She kept pouring champagne into his glass until no more came out of the bottle. She had had only the two glasses of it herself.

Around the now-sealed wound she wrapped gauze and held that in place with strips of zinc-oxide tape she tore off the roll.

"Try not to flex the arm or move it around a whole lot," she said.

He finished the last of the champagne in his glass. "I hadn't really thought of what we are doing as dangerous," he said.

"You mean other than earlier leaping off a moving car onto the back of this truck."

"Motorcycle. It was a motorcycle that gave me the catch-up ride."

"Really? I was thinking you'd jumped from the back of a pickup or something."

"I didn't have a lot of time to mull over my chances at the time."

"It's a wonder you're alive."

He sat there feeling warm and relaxed, not thinking about his arm at all as she put away the first aid things and cleaned up the table, slipping the empty champagne bottle into the trash bag with the bloody wrappings.

She leaned closer to look at his face. Her eyes seemed enormous at that range. Her skin looked so soft. He started to reach up with his good hand.

"We'd better get you to bed. Rest is the best thing possible for that arm. Besides, it's just starting to get light outside, and we'd better get out of sight in case the driver tries peeping in through the portholes."

He wanted to argue and maybe try to hold her. But he wobbled as he stood and let her lead him to the bed. He stretched out and closed his eyes for just a second but forgot to open them.

Chapter 16

*"I*nnocence, like virginity, is overrated," *Otto often said to Hardy at the gym.*

HARDY OPENED HIS EYES, and Ivy was bending closer to look at him. Her nose almost touched his. Her eyes seemed huge, enormous.

"How are you this morning?"

He could feel and hear the rasp of tires on asphalt. The truck was moving once more.

Last night, as his eyes were struggling not to close, he had had a thought. She still looked like a chipmunk, but she was the most beautiful one he'd ever seen. For a hazy second or two, he had figured that they really shouldn't sell stuff like that champagne to people if that was what it did.

In the morning, as his eyes opened wider, he had a second thought. *Nope, it wasn't the champagne.* She still looked amazing and wonderful to him. He almost reached out to her.

He had slept on his right side so his bandaged left arm could keep from getting jostled. Behind him something stirred.

"That's Frosty," Ivy said. "He insisted on climbing up in bed with you. There wasn't any room left for any Clara Barton or Florence Nightingale to get in too."

He sat up in the bed, his right hand going up to rub his chin. "I must look a mess."

"Too bad, because our Lothario of a driver probably got fed and showered last night or this morning, so it's likely any stops will be short and perfunctory."

Hardy started to get out of bed and winced.

"Here, let me help you." She reached out. "You should avoid using that arm for anything, or you'll set back what healing you've gained."

He felt the usual qualm about being helped and hesitated to let her help. He was used to fending for himself. But she opened her eyes wider at him, and he relaxed, shrugged, and let her take his arm.

She started to lead him to the small table.

"I want to look out the windows," he said. "It's why we're here."

"Okay. But I'm going to rig you up a sling, just for a day or two. Then that arm should be far enough along to heal on its own, as long as you don't do anything foolish."

He started to lower himself to the cabin floor without moving his hurt arm. But he wobbled and almost fell.

She stepped forward and caught him then helped him get all the way down.

"You like me needing you, don't you?" he asked.

"It's a change. But don't get used to it. I like you when you are your assertive, confident self. So just take it easy and heal."

Frosty came across the cabin to plop down beside him. He still had a slight limp.

"I've already fed and watered him. Is there anything I can get for you?"

"I'd love a cup of coffee just now."

"Sorry."

"Can you look over Frosty, see if he's okay?"

Ivy pulled the dog closer. He was reluctant to leave Hardy's side. She manually extended his legs, one by one. Then she felt along his ribs and back. Other than rolling his eyes back and wagging his tail when she ran her fingers across his back, he didn't show any response.

"He doesn't seem to be in pain. He's bouncing back."

"He might well have saved my life. A guy with a pipe was getting ready to swing at my head."

She suppressed a grin and didn't say whatever she was going to say. But she stayed amused even as she made a sling for his arm with a pillow case and a couple of safety pins.

"You don't have to wear it all the time, but it'll help you remember to take it easy with that wing," she said.

"Okay, because it's going to be a real pickle getting off the truck and back on with this thing."

Most of Arkansas was flat, and the land around them looked pretty much like that around any interstate highway. They did see an XXX sign in the distance near one ramp and could see a number of semi-trucks in the parking lot.

This part of the highway across the state proudly called itself the Arkansas Pig Trail. But Hardy didn't spot a single pig farm, so he supposed there were just the razorbacks in the woods.

Sitting calmly by a porthole, looking out, careful not to move his arm about, Hardy found himself particularly savoring the small joys of travel, glimpses of something different now and again. A lighthouse stood up from the edge of a small town, hundreds of miles from any ocean. An oyster bar was shaped like a large boat with glass windows on all sides.

Even the people in passing cars presented fresh and contrasting studies of mankind. In one vehicle, all the family members inside were glum and looking away from each other. In the SUV right after that, everyone was singing along with each other.

Then they began to see signs encouraging them to visit the Arkansas diamond mine.

"Do you think people are still really finding diamonds there, or is the mine salted as a tourist attraction?" Ivy sat on the other side of Frosty, whose head rested on Hardy's knee.

Hardy chuckled. "I'll bet it kills you not to be able to search the internet and find out."

"Stupid phone."

"Here's something to think about," he said. "Thousands of people visit that place each year, and most of them find nothing. But a couple times a year, just when a little publicity would boost the number of tourist visits, a big stone is found. Some people find that suspicious. Also, the worth of all the stones ever found isn't greater than the amounts paid to come look for diamonds. So, like Las Vegas, the mine still comes out ahead."

"You think they're cheating people?"

"Well, no. What people want is the *chance* to look for diamonds. I don't know enough about the place to know if they are salting the area or not, but even if they are, people get what they came for. They can say they've been diamond mining once in their lives."

"I must say you seem as fair and unjudgmental as a person can be."

"I try to maintain an open and unbiased mind."

For a stretch of the highway, the road around them was mostly the regular green directional signs and an occasional accident or traffic stop by a state trooper. Once, when traffic slowed way down, they soon found out why. An RV on the far side of the highway, in the lanes going the other direction, was on fire. A family stood a hundred feet away, watching a fire truck trying to contain a blaze that was shooting up twice the RV's height in yellow flames and billowing black smoke. One of the younger family members held a dog in his arms.

"I'm glad they got the dog out," Ivy said.

Just a few more miles along the highway, they slowed and started down a ramp.

"Seems a little early for a stop," Hardy said.

"Maybe the fuel that grand-theft dude used up decided him to make an earlier stop to fuel up."

"Or maybe that's the real reason." Hardy pointed at a sign: Boudreaux's Motel and Cajun Café.

"A mom-and-pop truck stop, not one of the big chains. This should be fun. If our driver sits down to a meal, we might have time for showers. But Frosty comes first."

As soon as they watched the driver, in a red shirt this time, head for the restaurant, Ivy started down the ladder first, carrying Frosty under one arm.

"Are you okay with that?" Hardy asked.

"He's lighter than he should be, by far. Thank goodness, in this instance."

Once on the ground, she went around and checked the truck's cab. She called up to Hardy, "Doors are locked, and keys are gone. Looks like he learned a lesson. He must have realized that at least he left the keys in the last time."

She held Frosty's leash, and they started off on a walk.

Hardy gripped his shaving kit in his teeth as he one-armed his way down the ladder and the back of the truck. Then he took off toward a big square building where a sign on one side said Showers.

He shaved and showered as quickly as he could, the shower especially tricky since he had to keep his bandaged left arm out of the water. He regretted putting on the same clothes again, but Ivy was in the same situation.

She was carrying Frosty back up into the yacht as he got back to the truck.

"My turn." Ivy reached to rub a hand in his wet hair and grabbed her purse. She was up and out of the cabin in a flash. By the time he got back onto the deck, she was halfway to the building for showers herself.

He had to admit she was holding up particularly well with their less-than-luxury conditions. Once back inside the cabin, he started cleaning. Old habits died hard. He'd kept the boat clean for so long that it pained him to see any clutter.

Frosty followed him around, fascinated by every movement and not willing to let Hardy out of his sight.

Once the cabin was as clean as he could get it, Hardy sat down at the breakfast nook table, resting his injured arm on its surface. He had felt good there for a few minutes when he had something he could do. Now, he had too much time to think.

He got up and went onto the yacht's deck, checked the fastenings holding the Zodiac in place, and looked for anything else that might be loose. If the driver came across the parking lot first, he would have to go below and lock the hatch. The guy was almost certainly on his toes after having left the truck unlocked overnight. He'd be even more rattled if he knew the truck had taken a brief jaunt. They were all lucky that had turned out as well as it had. He looked down at his arm in its sling. *Well, almost okay.*

He could see Ivy coming across the parking lot. A couple of potbellied truck drivers just getting out of an eighteen-wheeler saw her and moved closer. They all stopped to chat, then she stepped around them and kept coming.

One of the men looked like he might walk after her. But the other tugged on his arm, and they headed for the restaurant.

"What did those men want?" he asked when she had climbed up onto the deck. He watched for the driver.

"Oh, just a couple of road-lonely old dudes who think they are far cuter than they are. Why, are you feeling protective?"

"Kind of."

"Aw, that's cute too." She reached to his freshly shaved cheek and gave it a soft tweak.

She carried her bags down into the cabin while he locked the hatch behind her.

He joined her at the table. She took out two round Styrofoam containers, removed the lids, and put plastic spoons and paper napkins next to them. He leaned closer and took a sniff. Frosty was pressed close and at his side, trying to get to the smell too.

"Warm food for a change," Ivy said. "Gumbo, and I got a small sack of deep-fried okra as well."

"It does sound good." Hardy sat down. "I don't know how I'm ever going to repay you."

"Oh, don't you worry about that. There might come a time I get demanding about sexual favors or something on that order in return."

Hardy felt the blush that shot up from his neckline all the way to his hair.

"I'm kidding. Now, dig in." She dipped her spoon in her gumbo and began to eat delicately.

Chapter 17

They ate quietly, stopping for a second when they heard the driver check the yacht's hatch to ensure it was locked. He was being more careful. They had expected that.

The driver started the truck and took it over to the fuel pumps to fill it.

While he did that, Ivy slid the other bag closer.

"Oh, and I picked up this for you." She dug inside the bag and brought out a worn paperback copy of *The Adventures of Huckleberry Finn.* "By the front door, there was a small cart where drivers could drop off books they'd read and pick up ones they hadn't. You told me that the first thing Dana did when his ship met another ship was to try and trade books for new reading material."

He took it and looked inside. It was a facsimile edition of the original, just as it had appeared in its 1884 release, with the illustrations by E. W. Kemble. The pages were soft and here and there had been dog-eared and straightened again. Inside the front cover, someone had inscribed, "To Abigail on her 16th birthday. Love, Mom." Hardy wondered right away who Abigail was and why she had chosen not to keep it, and how many trucker hands the book had passed through until it arrived in his hands.

"I don't think I told you that about Dana," he said. "About him trading books when they met other ships."

"I must remember it from when I read the book once," she said.

"I wonder why Abigail let it go." He showed her the inscription.

"She may have thought it a boy's book. Some people do."

"Really?"

"I'll bet you liked *Robinson Crusoe* once too."

"I did when I was quite a bit younger. It was my favorite. But I can't even read Daniel Defoe at all anymore. He's far too preachy and a little boring."

"I can see why *Robinson Crusoe* would appeal to you when younger. It satisfies male dreams that are most vivid when young but never wholly go away."

"And what's that?" The gumbo was delicious, but his appetite was fading as an apprehension grew.

"Think of it as the desire to be fully self-sufficient. Crusoe builds his own private kingdom of which he is the sole leader, even after Friday arrives. It's an ideal world with no wife or children to usurp his authority. Lonely, but a heaven on earth, of sorts."

"And Dana's world?" he asked.

"He was at least a team player, a working member of a ship's crew. But with not a woman on board."

"Doesn't poor Huck fall into that boy's-book world?"

"You should eat your soup while it's warm. As for Huck, he went down that river the same way as we're taking our panoramic and picturesque slice through America. But he showed compassion and went against the prevailing views of the time to support and save Jim. He trusted his own heart and compassion and not the thoughts of others."

"But he had only aunts in his world, not even a Becky Thatcher."

"There is that one time when he dresses as a young girl, years before that would be considered a moment in drag," she said.

"Are you somehow saying that my past has shaped me too firmly into being some kind of self-sufficient loner?"

"No. We're just talking about literature here." She finished her soup and put her spoon down while frowning at his still half-full container.

"But I also got more batteries, so you can read it to me."

"I... I..." He supposed that was the sort of thing young women had to be careful about. Someone able to be alone, who wanted to be alone, and who could enjoy solitude enough that he wouldn't need or savor the presence of a chirpy girl like her, in the long term. Mostly, he felt confused. Just when he felt they were getting closer, he at the same time felt they had gotten suddenly distant. He wondered how much, if any, of that stemmed from her having to pay for everything, just at a time when he was questioning the balance of their being together.

"Look, if there's anything ulterior here," she said, "it's that I'm just trying to know you, understand what you're about. I mean, like this cell phone thing. Is it because you don't want to be connected... to any-one?"

"I don't mean to tell others how to live or be, or to even think that," he said. "It just makes me sad when others are glued to a tiny screen while all the things we're enjoying are rolling by."

"You don't even own one, though, or a wristwatch, for all that."

He put his spoon down. He didn't want to admit that he simply hadn't been able to afford either, a subject that emphasized the gap be-tween them.

"Please don't let that gumbo go to waste," she said, "and try the fried okra. We said we wanted to taste our path as we took it."

He wanted time to think. But damn, the food was good. He reached for a piece of okra and tried to grin, but even he knew it was a feeble grin. Still and all, he did finish eating, and she let him do all the cleaning up.

Through the rest of the day, they sat on opposite sides, looking out their portholes. He mostly watched passing families and tried to imag-ine the internal dynamics of each.

Alone. Together. Are people ever really happy?

When he had lived by the ocean, Hardy had gone down to the shore often to listen to the waves lapping at the sand and pilings. Al-ways, there were cars parked where they could be near the water, with guys, most often, sitting inside and reading newspapers, looking at their phones, or looking out across the ocean. He knew these were probably married men not wanting to go home at that moment but just wanting to sit somewhere else other than where they lived, where the wife or family was.

They had been having such a good time.

Frosty seemed confused. For a while, he went back and forth between them. Then he settled down beside Ivy, as if taking her side.

But there were no sides. It was all in Hardy's head. He sat and tried to sort out what was bothering him and why it was all his own fault.

The sky overhead grew gradually more overcast, turning the day into a grey-tinted painting of some pretty dreary-to-begin-with farmland and the same-old-same-old fast food signs marring what had once been gently rolling green hills and woods.

Just over the Oklahoma border, the truck pulled into a rest stop, one with bathrooms. Hardy had previously been looking forward to thinking about those Conestoga wagons poised at the border in 1889, waiting to surge across the former Indian territory to claim land, some of them getting the jump and being sooner.

Instead, a mild drizzle had started to fall. They waited for the driver to get back to the truck, check everything, and then climb back into his sleeper compartment before they dared walk Frosty and take advantage of the facilities.

Hardy couldn't shower, but he did manage to shave again. His usual apprehension was that he would be standing there, shaving at a sink, and the driver of their truck would walk in. But when he thought about it, the driver didn't know anything about Hardy and wouldn't recognize him if he saw him.

He looked down at his clothes. It sure would be nice to use a laundromat, but then he pictured himself sitting naked on a chair, waiting for his scanty belongings to be done. That was nothing to use as a postcard photo.

Ivy was still using his spare shirt as something to wear at night. She got into it that evening and made a bed on the floor with the blanket he had been using. "You can have the bed," she said.

Frosty went over and settled down beside her.

As he climbed onto the bed and got into a position favoring his healing arm, she said, "You know, you do pull your weight on this trip. We're equal partners whether you realize that or not."

He tried to fall asleep but lay awake for the longest time, eyes open and thinking—well, trying to think.

Did he feel she was emasculating him because he wasn't able to pay for food the way she was? Or was it because she had touched on his male tastes in literature, toward Bildungsromans at that, growing-up novels? Had being around a female exposed how much he was still growing up, not all the way fully baked yet? Well, who was? There was no shame in constantly learning, observing and growing. He suspected he would be doing it all his life. He *wanted* to be doing it all his life. After those thoughts had whirled around awhile, he started hearing a Bob Dylan line, "Anyone not busy being born is busy dying." That spun around like a warped vinyl record for a longish spell.

Then it began to rain in earnest, the drops slamming in sheets across the boat, making it a cozy and comforting place to be. His eyes closed in spite of himself.

Chapter 18

He was heading down the Mississippi River on the raft with Huck and Jim. Ahead, they could make out a waterfall, and they were going right toward it, faster and faster. The steering oar broke, snapped right off, and their frantic paddling wasn't even slowing them. They looked at each other with wide eyes. They got to the upper lip of the falls, where the muddy brown water was turning into a white frothy churn far below, and started over and downward...

HARDY WOKE TO THE SOUND of the truck's wheels rasping along on slightly damp asphalt. The rain had stopped, but the light outside the portholes was dim at best.

Ivy sat beside the starboard porthole, watching the flat countryside outside grow brighter.

Hardy glanced toward the breakfast nook. "I would give worlds for a cup of coffee just now."

"Is your arm feeling better?"

What he really felt was sheepish. He lifted his injured arm gently. "I can move it about now without feeling it might pop apart like a container of pop-apart rolls. Gosh, I'm sorry I mentioned them. Now I'm hungry."

"We'll be due for a truck stop visit before long," she said. "Our driver skipped breakfast, so I'm guessing he'll want to stop at one of these roadside diners I keep seeing go by. I wonder what the specialty food of Oklahoma is?"

"My money would be on chicken-fried steaks with mashed pota-toes, green beans maybe, and a fruit turnover."

"Oh my gosh." Her hand went to her stomach. "Now you've made *me* hungry."

He went over and eased down to sit beside her. "Hard to tell you were a cottage cheese fiend only a few days back."

"When you're only eating one meal a day..."

He reached out and took her hand and held it. She stopped speak-ing. Her eyes welled up with moisture.

"I'm sorry," he said. "I was spoiling what should be a good time to-gether. I'm prone to overthink, which in the land of the intuitive gets me into trouble. I get skittish and pop up deflector shields. I need to learn from Frosty to go with the flow."

She was suddenly in his arms, hugging him, then without knowing how it started, they were kissing, deeply and earnestly, none of that sec-ond-cousin stuff.

After a few minutes, they pulled back to arm's length but still held each other. Frosty wriggled close to their thighs, whining and wagging his tail.

Ivy's cute rounded cheeks were wet, and her eyes were red rimmed but open wide and fixed on him.

"What do we do now?" he asked.

"I can show you, but it might mean you miss a fair chunk of Okla-homa."

"That's okay. I've seen red dirt before."

He let her lead him over to the bed, where they both began to tug off their clothes and toss them on the floor. When Frosty tried to climb into the bed with them, Ivy pushed him firmly back toward the floor, where he curled up.

Then they turned toward each other again, and they were naked, pressed against each other, and kissing again with all the intensity and fireworks Hardy had ever experienced in his life.

They missed one stop the truck made, and they really needed water. But they gave the dog most of what they had, opened a bottle of the champagne, and climbed back in bed, where they spent most of the day.

The driver stopped again at one of the smaller, more folksy truck stops he seemed to favor when he could. This one said Red Hot on its logo sign and had an even bigger Good Food sign next to that, as if a lot packed with semi rigs didn't already attest to that.

Once they had Frosty walked and put back on board, they visited the convenience store and bought two twelve-packs of water. Ivy found she could place an order with the restaurant over the counter and then come back for it.

Hardy was waiting inside the yacht when she came down the stairs into the cabin with a bag he could smell from across the room.

"Oh, I just saw the wildest thing as I came across the parking lot," she said. "I was walking and heard a whirring buzz at my feet. I right away was thinking snake or a noisy scorpion or something nasty. It turned out to be a cicada buzzing around on its back. It must have just recently emerged from its shell. But wait a minute. Here's the crazier part. While I stood there, a mockingbird swooped in, spreading its wings, ignoring me, and went peck-pecking toward that cicada. The bug must have seen it because it flipped over and took off into the air, fast as it could go. The mockingbird lit out after it, and don't you know, it caught that cicada in midair and gulped it down. I couldn't believe it."

"I wish I could have seen that," Hardy said, "but at least you were there to be able to share the story. That's incredible. It's equivalent to me swallowing something the size of a football. I bet you'd pay to see me try to do that."

"Keep that thought in mind," she said. "I only got one order, but wait until you see it. We can split it."

She handed him the plastic forks and knives and opened a huge square Styrofoam container to reveal a mountain of hash browns half the size of a football, topped by two chicken-fried steaks smothered in brown gravy. A ring of green beans ran in a circle around the outside of the mound.

"That's one order?"

She nodded. "I decided to pass on the apple turnovers though they smelled heavenly. Our driver was over on the far side of the restaurant, digging into his meal like a starving longshoreman when he wasn't chatting up the waitress. He was far too busy to notice me."

"His evening activities must give him an appetite."

"You should know." She giggled then blushed all the way to her ears.

He couldn't comment because he was blushing too.

"I do wonder if all of our driver's little dalliances along the way don't result from him lining up a series of waitresses across America," she said.

"He is turning out to be quite a character," Hardy said.

When they had eaten all they could and let Frosty have the rest, they went back to looking out the windows. "I don't know if you know this," Hardy said, "but I just found out from a map on the store wall that the highway we're on, Interstate 40, is in places the out-and-out replacement for the old Route 66, which was once known as 'The Main Street of America.' In Steinbeck's novel *The Grapes of Wrath*, the highway was called 'The Mother Road,' and it was the escape route from the dust bowl. Route 66 has also been called 'The Will Rogers Highway.' So we are, after all, sometimes on the route your father wanted the yacht to sail on."

"Do you know what?"

"What?"

"You were doing so well at not being a font of trivia and bad jokes there for a stretch."

"Well, there's only one way to shut me up."

So she kissed him.

They looked out the porthole, and most of what they could see was flat land stretching out, more green highway signs, and clusters of fast-food franchises and occasional truck stops.

"I think we can afford to miss some of this," she said. She took his hand and led him back over to the bed.

SOME WHILE LATER, HE woke and took in her sleeping face and her lips and her hair, still a little damp from their sweaty activity. He ran a finger along her cheek and ended up cupping her under her chin with his hand.

Her eyes fluttered open, and she smiled. "Why did you reach down that time and pull me up on board? If you'd left me there, I would have found my way back home somehow."

"I didn't want to lose you."

"Have you ever lost someone?"

"I had a friend die on me before. Dave was a best friend. But I wasn't talking to him at the time someone ran him over. I didn't even go to the funeral."

"And you the kindest pirate on all the high seas. Why…? Oh. Does this have anything to do with the word *faithfulness* being on your list of desirable traits?"

"It might. But he was also a thief. It turned out he lifted things as well as stole people. He even stole from me once." That was how Hardy remembered the night of finding Dave with Claire.

"Did you hurt him?"

"No." He hadn't hurt her either, except to walk away. "But I wasn't the only one he stole from, and the next guy put the ultimate hurt on him. The guy he stole from there was a kind of passive-aggressive sort, but he owned a car."

"It's rare that justice or karma plays out. Did that make you feel better?"

"No. Not at all," he said. "What about you? Is finding someone who is a kind person important to you because you've been hurt or burned?"

"I'm afraid I had a thing for bad boys at one time."

"Did your father think that was to punish him?"

"Of course he did. But it wasn't. I was just girlish stupid. But I'm done altogether with that sort."

"One must have done something pretty awful."

"That depends on whether you count trying to sell someone to another guy for a six-pack of beer and a motorcycle that didn't even run."

"Ouch. You didn't go along with the deal?"

She gave his chest a shove that didn't move him at all. "I'm glad just to be back to a normal life."

"We're going across the country as illegal baggage on a truck. I don't think I'd call this normal."

Chapter 19

The truck slowed, and they felt it getting off the highway to go down another exit ramp.

"I didn't think we were scheduled for another stop," Hardy said.

Ivy chuckled. "You sound like you're on a train that sticks to such things as schedules and stops."

The truck went down a two-lane road for quite a ways, farther than the driver had ever taken the rig off the highway before. He turned to the right onto a road that wasn't paved at all. A parallel set of tire prints ran down the center of red dirt lined by bushes for a stretch then open wide fields, one with a red-tinted tin-roof cabin with no paint. Its silver wooden boards had been sanded smooth by the wind, and there were no windows or doors, just hollow openings where they had once been.

Hardy saw several red-tailed hawks sitting on fence posts or low tree limbs, claiming ownership to a territory where each could harvest mice, snakes, and any bobwhite or pheasant they could spot.

The truck slowed at last, though they couldn't see a house yet. Thick cattle fencing ran along the right of the road, and a chest-high barbed-wire fence ran along the left. In the middle of the left field, the sun reflected off the surface of a pond, the kind of stock tank ranchers use.

Then they saw the house, with a porch that went all the way around and pale-yellow siding with burgundy trim. A woman was standing on the porch, waving. They ducked back from the portholes so that she couldn't see them. But they could have spared themselves the effort. Her eyes stayed fixed on the truck's cab.

She looked like the sort of woman who might well be a waitress at some spot the driver had frequented in the past, a thick woman of hardy pioneer stock who nevertheless was beaming as the driver climbed out of his cab, carrying his bag. He melted into her open arms as they met.

Hand in hand, they started off toward the house.

"Now, let's take a look around and see what kind of place we've landed in this time," Ivy said.

Frosty zoomed back and forth through the cabin, eager to get out into the night air. They lowered him down to the ground, and Ivy took the end of his leash. "Let's see what's over here behind this thick steel-pipe fence. It's thick enough they could keep rhinos in it."

"No matter what you do, someone has been there and done that," Hardy said. "If you were to put a rhino in your backyard, someone would say, 'Oh, we used to have a rhino.'"

"Let's just see," she said.

The sky was dimming as they approached the fence, but the moving shapes on the far side of the pasture began to take shape, and they started toward the fence when they saw them.

As they got closer, Hardy could make out the herd and reckoned there might well be three to four hundred of them. "Ostriches," he said. "Someone's farming ostriches. Don't get too close to the fence."

"Why?"

"They peck, and at anything shiny. They'd just as soon go for your eye as your wrist watch."

"So we shouldn't walk Frosty in that direction. Let's see what's on the other side."

The fence wasn't so rigorous along the pasture on the other side of the lane. Three-strand barbed-wire ran along a series of wooden fence posts. Creatures were stirring behind it as well.

Frosty seemed more interested in them.

"Llamas," Ivy said. "I guess simple cattle farming wasn't enough for this woman."

He could see five or six of them. More were probably out of sight.

"I believe I see the Dolly Llama," Hardy said. "And there's a mama llama with a baby llama."

"And beyond that?"

"A pond, or livestock tank as they call them in the Southwest."

"Sure looks tempting."

"I think we'll be safer there than with the ostriches."

Dark was settling in so quickly that in a few more moments, they might not have been able to see the pond.

Hardy climbed the fence first. Ivy helped him get Frosty under it when Hardy lifted the lower strand of the barbed-wire fence. Then Ivy clambered over to join him.

Near a fence, he often thought of Robert Frost's poem and nearly said, "Good fences make good neighbors," but he kept that to himself since it was far from apt at the moment.

"I don't know what the llama equivalent of cow pies is, but I'd keep an eye out for them," he said. The sky was almost black by the time they started across the field. Stars were showing, and a full moon slid out from a cloud to light the nearest objects.

Frosty led the way and ensured they stepped on nothing but dirt and grass until they came to the edge of the pond. One end had a concrete rim, like a dam, that held the water in. Hardy went in that direction.

The llamas seemed content to leave them alone and keep their distance. Perhaps the presence of Frosty made them wish to be elsewhere.

At the dam, Ivy started tugging off her clothes until she stood slim and wonderfully naked in the moonlight. She sat down and eased off the concrete into the water, proving that it was a good thing she hadn't dived in, when the water came only to her chest. She dipped down into it and rose again to glisten wetly.

Hardy handed her the leash, and Frosty dove in to swim toward her.

He knew he couldn't get his injured arm wet. Who knew what germs might be in the water, though it looked clean and clear to him? He took off his clothes and eased in until he could rest his bandaged arm on the dam.

Ivy dove under the water and disappeared. Frosty started to thrash around, looking frantically for her until he felt the tug on his leash and she came up again and swam. He paddled to her and stayed at her side as she frolicked and splashed, not daring to giggle or call out lest they be discovered.

Hardy washed himself with his good hand, taking advantage of the bathing moment. Ivy seemed to be having all kinds of fun, and that gave him a warm rush to his toes and fingers.

He stood in waist-deep water when she waded over to him, trailing Frosty behind.

"This is just the sort of thing we needed," she said.

"The joke would certainly be on us if this lady friend sent him packing instead of letting him stay the night and he took off without us."

"I don't know if I would chuckle long over that," she said.

"I put my faith in our driver. I'm betting we don't see or hear from him again until dawn."

As they waded up out of the pond, the water got shallower until they stood beside the dam.

Ivy's slim body glistened in the moonlight.

He wanted to give her a hug, say things to her, and do things to her. But he stayed quiet as she tugged on her clothes. He did the same, feeling them cling to his damp body.

They started back across the field, the llamas moving to the pond behind them, as if they had been waiting for the intruders to leave.

They looked in all directions and crossed over the lane to climb back up and get Frosty aboard as well. Hardy locked the hatch.

The cabin was lit by moonlight beaming in through the portholes.

Coming down the stairs, he saw that Ivy was dripping as she crossed the cabin. He would clean that up in the morning.

He made sure Frosty's water bowl was full. "Now what?"

"Now you read to me." She tugged off her things and started hanging them up to dry. Naked, she went over and got his spare shirt and put it on. He tugged off his wet clothes and hung them up to dry as she had, where they couldn't be seen by anyone peeking through the portholes. Then he put on his gym shorts and tank top. She was already in bed, holding the Twain book and his flashlight.

Frosty curled up on the floor below the bed.

Ivy snuggled close to Hardy, who turned on the flashlight, opened the book, and began to read.

He read on until he had Huck and Jim heading down the mighty Mississippi on their raft, looking up at the sky speckled with stars above them. Then Jim said the moon probably laid them, and Huck allowed as how he had seen a frog lay most as many.

Ivy reached over and dog-eared the page's corner and closed the book.

Hardy turned off the light and lowered it and the book to the cabin floor, getting a lick on the hand from Frosty in the process.

He turned toward Ivy, and their lips found each other in the dark with no effort at all.

Chapter 20

Sometimes when he went to describe something that gave him so much joy and happiness, he realized that all the really good clichés had already been taken and used. It looked like he was going to have to coin some new clichés.

HARDY WOKE UP AND REALIZED he had ended up on the far side of the bed. His bandaged left arm was curled around the nude, sleeping Ivy. *I could get used to this,* he thought.

Light was growing brighter outside the portholes as dawn eased over their tiny spot in the world.

The truck's engine started. In moments, they were rolling along once more, heading toward the ramp to get back to the highway and to live up to Horace Greeley's advice to "Go west, young man."

"Oh my gosh." Ivy jumped out of bed and started tugging on her clothes. "We'd better get to our portholes, or we'll miss most of Oklahoma altogether."

"You can always get the video of the musical." Hardy slid across the bed and got up. He started looking around for his pants.

Frosty had been curled up on them but got up and wagged his tail eagerly while nuzzling their thighs and sniffing them over.

As they got to a porthole, Hardy could see the sky was dimming around them. But he could still see fields and barns and buildings as parts of mostly flat Oklahoma rolled by. Only here and there did he see small mounds of hills, looking like a carpet that had bunched up in places.

Ivy held his hand, and Frosty tried to wriggle his way between them but had to settle for sprawling across their knees.

"We need to capture and keep experiencing the magic," Ivy said. "Whether you know it or not, whether this was on purpose or an accident, this was a very good idea. Maybe we're seeing the tip of the iceberg of this sprawling, vast country, but it makes me want to feel and see even more, and that's a very good thing."

The truck slowed and entered an off-ramp and started down its gradual slope toward a rest stop.

The day was easing into that awkward time of dusk when the sky seemed neither light nor dark. Objects could be seen less clearly, and the illusionary vagueness of the inside shadowy corners of buildings might lead those disposed to believing in ghosts or fairies to imagine seeing them.

Hardy wasn't one of those, but he did hope the limited visibility would help them make the most of a stop that might be only moments long. The driver left the truck's engine running.

They waited until the driver had left the cab and was out of sight before Hardy helped Ivy carry Frosty down to the ground level. He watched her walk the dog to the far end of the stop, where they wouldn't be spotted. He checked the cab's doors and was glad to find that the driver had at least locked the truck this time. Then he climbed back up and waited for his turn.

The driver came out of the men's room far quicker than Hardy had expected. He was hoping Ivy would realize that and start back toward the truck. She was almost out of sight.

The driver didn't head right back toward the truck. He looked toward the ladies' restroom then looked right and left. Hardy didn't know if the driver could see Ivy or, at the least, a female form, but he took off in a stroll in Ivy's direction.

There was nothing Hardy could do to warn her. She might recognize the red shirt and try to avoid him if there was any place to go, but there wasn't.

All too soon, the driver came back toward the truck. He was whistling to himself. Hardy was poised to dash to the hatch and get inside and lock it, but the driver waived his usual check of the yacht's deck.

The truck's cab door closed. They had only a minute or so.

Ivy and Frosty came running up to the back of the truck.

Hardy climbed down and helped as best he could with one good arm to get them up into the back of the truck just as it shifted into gear and started to roll forward.

They clambered the rest of the way up the yacht's ladder but waited until they were down inside the cabin to talk.

"Whew," Hardy said.

"We barely made it." Ivy was still breathing hard. "I thought we had longer than we did."

"Our driver is unfathomable. But I still think he's a pip."

Ivy raised one eyebrow into a question.

"He follows his own whim and experience of past drives back and forth across the country." Hardy shook his head. "He may well be a rake, but for all that, I think I like the guy. I don't know anything about him, but I sense his likability. The string of waitresses across America must feel the same. He's a slow and careful driver, and he is vigilant about his load."

"In spite of having stowaways and getting his truck stolen once?" she asked.

"He's just not exceptionally bright."

"No brain surgeon, eh?"

"Not likely. He probably thinks the hippocampus is a college on the Nile."

"Now you're being too clever, like those schoolmates of yours back in Connecticut."

"Touché. Point taken."

"I wonder if we could have gotten by with all we have, had we had a normal professional driver and not one with other things on his mind."

"We're lucky he didn't see you," Hardy said.

"But he did."

"What? He saw you?"

"Of course he did. He came at me like a magnet zooming toward an iron pole."

"Did he say anything?"

"Can you believe it? He hit on me."

Hardy felt a quick flash of anger ripple through him.

Now, wait a minute. Am I suddenly feeling jealous or protective? What's up with that? A minute ago, he'd been saying how he liked their driver. *Don't go all caveman on yourself. Big Hardy going to protect tender little Ivy.* Well, he would. But that was beside the point. He pushed the thoughts away and shook his head. Without admitting to any emotions, he said, "Well, that means he was true to the character I imagine him to be. What's he like?"

"He's stocky, but not as potbellied as some of the truck drivers we've seen, and he's got this Elvis confidence sort of thing going on. He even gets a little lip curl as he speaks. 'You're a perty little *thing*. If you're feeling *lonely tonight*, I can stay a little *longer* here.' He talks like he's reading out song lyrics. His hair is receding, and he's got that bit of a paunch, but he's game to play all the way. When I told him no thanks, he said, 'Maybe some other time, *honey*,' and he headed back toward the truck. I had to hustle like anything to get back to the truck. Luckily, old Frosty can still move right along now that he's over his limp."

"Maybe that sort of patter works for our driver with some of the waitresses."

"They've got to be pretty desperate or starved for some loving," Ivy said.

"I suspect many are just that."

"At least he took my 'no means no' with a modicum of grace. Like you said, there's an easygoing likeability about him, but he is on the prowl nonstop, from what I can tell."

"Well, you've been seen by him now. You'll have to be careful he doesn't see you again miles from here. That would really make him cautious. Maybe he'd try to check the boat more carefully."

"He doesn't have a key to the hatch, does he?"

"No. Only your dad and I have keys. But we don't want him to start peeping in through the portholes. Who knows what he'd see."

She giggled then shook her head. "My heart's still beating fast. And I just about did Frosty in, rushing him back to our boat." She reached down to rub Frosty's head. He wagged his tail and looked up at her.

With her head tilted downward, Ivy looked over at Hardy. "By the way, did you know your ears flush pink when you're a little angry... or jealous?"

"Don't either."

"Do too."

As the night settled its dark blanket across most of Oklahoma, with only a glitter of red or green neon in the distance rolling by, they lay with their backs on the teak deck with Frosty beside them as they looked up at all the stars and the half moon.

"I know you probably know all about the phases of the moon," she said. "Thank you for not sharing that info dump with me. I just want to stare up at the moon and stars right now."

"I don't mean to sound like a know-it-all or a fountain of trivia. With me, raw curiosity outweighs displaying what I think I know. Because there's always a lot more I don't know."

"Aw, I was just ribbing you."

"If it's getting physical you want..."

"Maybe a bit later. I want to think about the stars awhile, to ponder about how far away they are."

"Fine with me," he said. They held hands, but Frosty managed to nudge his way between them, his back to Hardy and his paws embracing Ivy.

"It seems like we've had a dog forever," Hardy said.

"It feels like we've been on this trip forever," she said, "and I hope it never ends."

Chapter 21

Hardy and Ivy stayed quiet for a mile or two.

"Oh!" She squeezed his arm. "I just saw a shooting star."

"Good."

"Why is that good?"

"Because I saw it too and thought I might have imagined it."

"I have moments when I want to pinch myself as well," she said, "and don't take that as an invitation."

"I wish I knew enough about the stars so that if I look up from some other place I could know how they are different from there," he said, "places like the Caribbean, Iceland, or Australia."

"Do you have big travel plans for someday?"

"It would be great if I could sail to all those places."

"Hardy, have you lived on your own for long?"

"Since I was done with high school at seventeen."

"Didn't your—"

He headed her off before she could mention parents. "I had to work a spell to make enough to pay for my college. Because it was *my* money I went through in three years. But at least I don't have giant school loans to pay back."

"Three years, and you were your class valedictorian? That must be why those guys had so much love for you."

"I have never tried to make anyone angry about anything. But I have had people, like those guys, project their discomfort about themselves at me, as if I were responsible. I don't fully understand that sort of thinking, but I've seen it."

The wind that swept across them was getting cooler by degrees. Hardy felt a delicate quiver in Ivy's arm. "What do you say we go inside?"

Sometime in the night, he heard the driver pull over. Hardy didn't even get up to see where they were parked, especially since that would have meant disturbing Ivy and possibly stepping on Frosty. He let his eyes close again.

In the morning, the light was coming in the two open portholes, and the truck was rumbling along on the highway. Hardy glanced out the porthole just in time to see that a Welcome to Texas sign loomed ahead on their right.

"We kind of missed a lot of that last state," Ivy said. "To do Oklahoma justice, you might have to come back through sometime again."

"I don't know. I found it pretty memorable."

"In fairness, Texas doesn't look much different from the part of Oklahoma we just passed through. It sure is a flat state."

"Up here it is," Hardy said. "But Texas is so big it has mountains like the Guadalupe Mountains near the Big Bend in the far west, rolling up-and-down hill country to the west of Austin, tall timber country in the piney woods that run along its east side from Nacogdoches to Houston, Sonora desert country in the southwest, swampy land along the Louisiana border, and coastal areas along the Gulf of Mexico. Whatever you're in the topographical mood for, you can get it somewhere. We'll just be going through the panhandle, the shortest way possible across a state I'd like to see more of."

"Sounds like you've nosed around at the idea more than a little."

He nodded. "Enough to know we're going to be, at best, a six-hour drive north of the Alamo and any Davy Crockett dreams we might have about that. The rest of the way to the southern tip of Texas would be probably twice that, or more than a day's travel for our driver."

"Especially if there was a friendly, willing waitress along the way."

"There's that," Hardy said. "But we would sure get to see a wide variety of landscape."

She looked out the porthole. "I did think we would at least see some cattle ranches, but no."

Hardy could see oil rigs across a field they were passing, and the rockers were going, still drawing crude oil up from the ground.

They passed a barn that stretched out until it was longer than a series of warehouses. In a row in front of it were big round bundles taller than a man. They were wrapped, some in yellow, others in blue, but the centers were white, so they weren't straw or hay. Other bundles were bound rectangles.

"What the heck are those big ones?" Ivy asked.

"I think they're cotton. They must bale them in the bigger sizes the way hay is done these days."

A few bushes still stood along the edge of a cleared field they passed. They were speckled with white puffs of cotton the big machine picker had missed.

"There you go," Hardy said. "Cotton fields, at least harvested ones."

"Those modern bales are going to play hob with that song that says, 'Pick a bale of cotton, pick a bale a day.' These would sure mean a long day."

"Or a shorter one for a machine that can replace a hundred pickers."

"As long as we're on that theme, how long is a cotton-picking minute?"

"I think we're about to change the subject," Hardy said, "and talk about food." He pointed at a bright-yellow billboard just ahead.

The first words he had read on it were "FREE 72-oz Steak."

"Holy cow. That's a four-and-a-half-pound piece of meat."

"Steer really, not cow."

She frowned at him. "Still, it's free?"

"Here's the thing. I've heard about this Amarillo spot. It's only free if you follow the rules. You've got to eat the whole meal in under an hour. That includes the steak, a shrimp cocktail, a baked potato, a salad, and a roll with butter."

"I don't see that happening by me."

"Then you'd better get ready to shell out seventy-two dollars."

"I don't see that in the fine print," she said. "And I sure hope our driver doesn't try, or he's going to need a day-long nap."

"Also, you lose if you throw up during the hour you have to eat it all."

"I would throw up when they brought it to the table."

"There's a myth that the ancient Romans had a room called a vomitorium where, during a big feast, they could go to make room for more eating. But really, a vomitorium was a passage below a tier of seats in an amphitheater so big crowds could leave quickly at the end of a performance."

"Hardy?"

"Yeah?"

"Do you remember that chat we had about sometimes sharing too much?"

"Got it. Zipping it up over here."

But she chuckled and gave his shoulder a soft shove.

Traffic slowed for a spell as the truck passed through the middle of Amarillo. The truck rolled right past the American Quarter Horse Hall of Fame as well as the Big Texan Steak Ranch. Their driver kept his calm, steady pace, and soon, they were out the other end and rolling west.

"Thank heavens he didn't stop for that steak challenge," Ivy said.

"I'm hoping he'll decide to stop somewhere," Hardy said. "We've sure talked about food a lot. But I am feeling bad that I can't chip in on that."

"Don't. You've saved the boat from thieves and even saved me a time or two. I think you're more than pulling your weight on this boat trip."

"I was hoping we might catch a glimpse of the Cadillac Ranch. It should be around here somewhere." He went over to the other side's porthole. "Nope. Can't see it from here either."

"That's where a bunch of Cadillacs in rows are stuck nose first into the ground. Why would that interest you?"

"They were put there to baffle the public and at the same time represent America's conflicting dreams of art and business, not to mention tail fins sticking up in the air. I think it used to be visible from the old Route 66, but we'd have to take the frontage road and get off the highway. I doubt we could convince our driver to do that any more than stop to see a giant ball of string."

The starboard side was getting less interesting once the sprinkling of oversized hotels and motels at the edge of town died out. Hardy moved over to peek out the port side to see what was happening among their fellow highway travelers.

"Oh my," Ivy said.

Hardy moved back to her side to look out and saw a deer kneeling like a Sphinx to the right of the road. She had been hit and was sitting up, but her legs and body were bloody. Her mouth was open, and she was breathing hard. Blood was on her mouth too.

Ivy reached up to brush at a wet cheek.

Hardy felt as if his stomach had been punched. "There's nothing to do in that case. One fellow was even arrested once for stopping to put a hurt deer like that out of its misery. He was cited for shooting a deer out of season even though he hadn't tried to take it home or anything."

"Why?"

He looked at her.

"Do you suppose the arresting officer decided that the man who happened to have a rifle wasn't just being a Good Samaritan?" she asked.

"I don't know what the officer was thinking. We live in a time of suspicion of motives. Maybe he'd had a number of guys say they were helping a hurt deer when they had really wanted the meat. It's a muddle and perhaps based on past experiences of the officer. I even catch myself sometimes being suspicious and wary at first of people who say they want to help."

"Yet you've been helped and have helped others yourself, as recently as on this trip."

"You're right," he said. "My bacon has been saved more than once. But in the big picture, I have to fight a bias, too, because I think some of the greatest evil that goes on these days is when someone uses the impression of doing an act of good to benefit themselves. I know about some charities that rake a big cut for themselves, and others don't. When disasters happen, there are always some people who swoop in, not to help, but to take advantage. No matter who it is, doing anything like that is one wicked bad moral compass at work."

She rubbed her cheek dry and looked at him. "Anything personal in that you want to share?"

Hardy shook his head and looked back out the porthole.

He had been in his second year of college when he heard that the Sandersons had been arrested, all their files taken, and massive criminal charges were being brought against them. After all they'd done to take advantage of him and do harm to all the other kids at their orphanage, he didn't know how to feel: elated, vengeful, or just plain sad about something that seemed to have happened a long, long time ago. The only thing he didn't feel was surprised.

A few more miles along the highway, they saw two does with fawns eating safely on the other side of a seven-foot-tall wire-mesh deer fence.

"At least *they're* safe," Ivy said.

Just like that, the mood was less grim, and they were back to enjoying the panorama of the Texas Panhandle going by outside the yacht.

In a greener stretch of pasture they approached, a gust of breeze sent the blades of a windmill into motion to pump water up into a big metal tank. From the far side of the field, horses lifted their heads at the sound and broke into a gallop toward the tank, their manes and tails flowing out behind them.

Neither said anything, but Ivy reached out a hand for his and gave it a squeeze.

Chapter 22

"*A ranch cowhand usually had a string of horses to rotate and have a fresh one to use. But I've heard that a good cowboy always preferred to ride the horse that had a few quirks and challenged him the most.*"

"*Are you calling me a horse?*"

"*You know what I'm saying.*"

"*Well, the minute you strap on spurs, you'd best get ready for some fierce resistance.*"

THEIR DRIVER FINALLY did pull into a truck stop, one of the larger, sprawling kind with a sign that said Free Showers, which was a welcome sight to Hardy. He reached up to feel the rasp of stubble on his chin. The place looked like it had a good restaurant, too, from the number of other trucks pulled close to it, so he hoped that would keep the driver busy for a spell.

"You go first," he said to Ivy as soon as they saw the driver slip out of sight among the rows of parked trucks.

"This is turning out to be more fun than I expected," Hardy said to Frosty once they were alone. "Well, to be fair, I didn't even expect to be on a trip like this. But I'm glad you're along too. Maybe I *will* have to add Steinbeck's *Travels with Charley* to my reading list."

Frosty looked up at him and wagged his tail in a way that always made Hardy think the dog understood more than he let on.

Hardy kept the hatch locked and stayed inside. He would've liked to be up on the deck with the dog, but he couldn't risk getting spotted.

One thing he did notice was that a lot more than eighteen-wheelers rolled in to park near the restaurant. They were seventy or so miles from the New Mexico border, and the families and small groups climbing out of cars and trucks that had come from all directions seemed to know about the restaurant.

A few guys loitered around in groups outside, talking and watching the coming and going of restaurant patrons. Some looked like workers on a lunch break, while others looked like locals who had decided this was a good place to hang out. They picked at their teeth with toothpicks or smoked cigarettes.

Ivy came back after almost forty minutes. She was carrying a white plastic bag from the restaurant. As Hardy went to help her get Frosty down to the ground for his walk, she said, "You'd better scoot. I didn't mean to take so long. I can get Frosty down and back up again on my own."

"Okay." Hardy headed for the men's showers at a near jog.

As he approached the truck stop's cluster of central buildings, four young guys pushed off from a railing where they were all leaning. Three were lanky tall, and the other was round and short. They seemed the type who might have called each other to see what the others were wearing, because they all looked so alike. Each wore jeans with a crease ironed down the front, boots, shirts with pearl buttons, and all of it topped off with straw cowboy hats with the sides turned up and the front brim pulled down low to shadow their eyes. The only difference among their clothing was that one shirt was denim, another royal blue, and one tiny red and white checks, while the fourth specimen, the roundest, wore a fading burgundy shirt. As they went past, Hardy saw that each had a round circle in the right back pocket from a can of snuff or some other smokeless tobacco. Their faces varied enough that they didn't look anything like siblings. Maybe they were going to some sort of dance later.

He didn't give it much more thought. He rushed through shaving and grabbing a quick shower, wishing once more that he had a fresh change of clothes. But Ivy was in the same fix. There were washers and dryers at some of the truck stops, but they didn't have enough time to use them, and they weren't free. The shower was only free at this one if the truck's driver had bought more than fifty gallons of fuel. But no one was monitoring the shower area, so he just went ahead and used one of the showers as quickly as he could.

Hardy came out of the truck stop's showers, his hair still a little wet. He carried his shaving kit.

Ahead of him, he saw the back of the red shirt of their truck's driver as he was just walking away from the restaurant. Not good. Hardy eased closer to the nearest parked truck so that he could duck and hide if the driver looked back.

Then he heard barking.

He had never heard Frosty bark, but somehow, he knew it was their dog making the racket.

The driver walking ahead of him didn't respond to the noise, but Hardy knew Ivy was probably doing everything she could to quiet the dog. He ran out and around three trucks and could see Ivy climbing down the back of the truck with Frosty as he got closer. The four guys he'd seen earlier were standing not far from her. She and the dog took off at a jog, Frosty barking at the young men as they followed and started to close in.

Hardy ran as fast as he could until he went around the stalking guys and came up beside Ivy. They were out of sight of the yacht.

"These guys were trying to climb up onto the yacht." She pointed at the four men, who kept walking toward her.

Frosty barked at them and pulled at the leash she held.

"I had to get Frosty off before the driver figured out what was going on," she said.

He handed her his shaving kit and stepped to stand between her and the approaching men. "Go back to the truck. You should be okay now."

"What about you?"

"Just go."

She hesitated.

"If only to quiet Mr. Barky here before our driver sees you," he said.

She nodded and led Frosty away until he was out of sight and quit barking.

"Well, what do we have here?" said the guy in the blue denim shirt. "You gonna protect that gal all by your little own self?" He stared down at Hardy's bandaged left arm.

"If I have to. Why don't you just drop it and leave us be?"

"What? And miss the only bit of fun we've had coming our way all day?"

The other three guys chuckled and spread out. They looked just the young predatorial sort of lads who saw a frail-looking female by herself as an opportunity for them to be bad—very bad.

Hardy was reading their eyes. The shorter one in the faded burgundy shirt was stockier, maybe muscle or maybe fat. His piglike slits of eyes glittered eagerly and said he was the most eager to leap in and do harm the moment he could. He would be the first of them with whom Hardy had to deal.

Without another word, they rushed him.

Hardy spun and kicked at the right knee of burgundy shirt, catching him a firm blow with all his weight.

The guy crumpled to the ground, screaming, "Get him! Get him! Beat the little bastard into a puddle!"

The other three had slowed for a moment but began to press closer again, being more wary.

From the left, out from behind the nearest truck, an enormous dark blur rushed in.

A huge black man was suddenly among them, swinging his arms like a mother bear protecting her cubs.

The swat of one giant club of an arm knocked the one in the denim shirt to the ground, his hat sailing off in the other direction.

A backhand blow lifted the one in the royal-blue shirt up through the air to land on his butt a few feet away.

He grabbed the one in the checked shirt and threw him in the air far enough for him to bounce off the side of a parked semi trailer and crumple down onto the asphalt.

"Grrr." The black man went into an Incredible Hulk stance and flexed his chest and arms, eager for more.

The three most agile of the attackers scrambled to their feet and rounded up their hats. Two of them got on either side of their stout friend and helped him to his feet. The one who'd felt the metal side of a truck was limping but already heading off by himself.

"Get him. He's just a ni—" Burgundy Shirt started to yell.

One of those helping him clamped a hand over his mouth. "Shut up or you'll rile him worse than he is."

"Yeah, don't say it, dude, or you'll make him madder than he is," the denim-shirt friend said.

With an arm over each of their shoulders, he hobbled along as all of them moved away as fast as they could go, not looking back once.

The black man stood up straight and towered over Hardy. "Did you like that growl part? I use it on my kids."

"Thank you," Hardy said. He held out a hand.

"I'm Maurice LaVeck," the man said as he shook Hardy's hand with his, which was at least the size of a catcher's mitt.

"Did you play football?"

"Yes I did, at Southern Miss. I was an offensive lineman. I'm six foot seven and three hundred and twenty pounds, down from my playing weight, but the good eating along the way keeps me happy and hefty." He laughed again. "I was big enough to go pro if I wasn't a touch too slow. So I became a road scholar instead and drive a truck now. It's a sweet life, but my wife keeps trying to put me on a diet." He pointed at the semi rig beside them, with a big well-polished candy-apple-red cab that glittered in the sun. "I got me a Mack truck with a custom-rigged sleeper big enough for someone my size."

He must have read something in Hardy's face. "But I'm not inviting you inside or anything. It still barely holds me." His shoulders shook as he laughed.

"Well, thanks again."

"Hey, I was just paying it forward. Everyone needs a little help sometimes."

"Why?"

"There are forces, rhetoric, and biases trying to divide us all, so we can be more readily conquered," Maurice said. "It's up to us to help each other and get along. That sends a message though, unfortunately, some people will always refuse to understand."

Hardy glanced in the direction of the yacht on its truck. He couldn't see it from where he stood, which at least meant their driver couldn't see him.

"I don't mean to be short," he said. "I've got to go, or I'll miss my ride."

"No need to apologize for being short." Maurice chuckled to himself. Just about everything seemed to amuse him. "Nor about size. Our kicker, who was about your build, used to say, 'Size doesn't matter. It's not how big you are—it's whether you have a cute way of getting on and off.'"

"We're not talking about fighting now, are we?"

"Nope." Maurice laughed again. He winked. "I saw that little girl carrying down to the ground that dog that looked almost as big as she was."

"Well, bye." Hardy waved and spun to take off running while the big man climbed up into his rig.

Just as he'd feared, he could hear the truck's engine going. Ivy stood up on the yacht's deck, her eyes open wide in panic. The driver shifted into gear, and the truck started to roll forward.

Hardy was running as fast as he could, but he wasn't going to make it.

Then a semi with a big red cab pulled in front of the yacht transport truck. Their driver had to hit the brakes.

Hardy made it the rest of the way and scrambled up the back like a one-handed monkey.

Ivy rushed to put her arms around him. "You made it. Oh, you made it."

They both turned to look at the red cab of the truck that was now backing out of their driver's way. Maurice was giving their driver an apologetic look.

As their truck started forward again, they looked down at Maurice. He waved at them, and Hardy waved back.

Ivy waved too. "I'm guessing that man had something to do with you being unscathed."

"Yep. And those guys who were out to give you a hard time will have a real story to tell tonight, though not the one they intended, but just as ripping good."

Chapter 23

As they went down into the cabin, Frosty rushed over to Hardy and put his front paws on his chest, wagging his tail and trying to lick Hardy's face.

"I owe you a big thanks too, Frosty," Hardy said. "You were all about protecting us. I didn't even know you could bark. Just don't do it again when our driver is around. Okay?" He rubbed Frosty's furry white cheeks and patted him on his sides.

"Oh, and I have another good surprise for you," Ivy said.

She went over to the fridge and took out the white plastic sack she had been carrying earlier. "I got us lunch. I had to hide it because someone here was trying to get at it."

She slid the usual square white Styrofoam box out of the sack and put it onto the breakfast nook table.

Ivy grinned and flipped open the lid.

Hardy bent closer. "Ah. Beef ribs."

"This is probably the reason your rescuer stopped at this truck stop," she said.

"His name was Maurice, and I'll never forget him. He didn't need to step in and help, but he did. I wish I could do something back for him."

Ivy sighed. "I've been trying to tell and show you this all along, Hardy. Giving has no conditions."

He tilted his head and thought about it for a moment. "That's what Maurice said to me, only in different words. He kind of said that we're in a world where people should help each other more and hurt each other less."

"He sounds like a very wise man," Ivy said.

"I believe he was, and I certainly wouldn't want to arm wrestle him."

She looked up at him, and her eyes grew more intense. "There's a lesson here, and one particularly apt for you. Learning to give may seem the hardest lesson. Learning to receive is harder."

"Yes, ma'am." He resisted looking around her to stare at the beef ribs. *Is there potato salad and slaw in there as well?* He did put out a hand to keep Frosty from climbing up onto the table.

"Okay. Fortune cookie time is over," she said. "Let's eat. And don't you ever call me ma'am again."

"No, ma'am. I won't."

She gave his shoulder a shove, and they sat down at the table.

They ate quietly and with the intensity of hungry people coming across really good and tasty food. They had to keep Frosty from climbing up until they had the first rib bone cleaned enough to hand it down to him. Then he curled up on the cabin floor with the bone between both paws and chewed on one end of it.

When they were back at a porthole, watching the rest of Texas go past, Ivy leaned her head against Hardy's chest. "Sometimes, I think we live in a world that has some awful aspects to it."

"Like what?"

"Like those guys back there. They wanted to mess with me just because they are males and I'm a smaller female. At first, I thought they wanted the lark of a ride on the boat like us, but then I saw the lust in their eyes and a little anger. Maybe they're mad at some other girls for not being nicer to them and were going to take it out on me."

"You're probably right about that. They did seem to up to no good."

"Have you ever beaten a woman?" she asked.

"At what?"

She chuckled in spite of herself.

"You don't seem the type to ever do wrong by a woman."

"I admit to being loyal to a fault and prone to be far too trusting."

"I'm not talking about your past. I mean the kind of world we live in."

"Like what?"

"That swimmer at Stanford, for instance, who took advantage of a female who had passed out by a dumpster. He ended up convicted of three felony counts, and only two Swedish students pulling him off her kept him from doing more."

"I read about that."

"And do you know what steams me most about the whole thing?"

"All of it?"

"No. I mean the part about his father writing a letter to the judge, saying that the six-year prison term the prosecution wanted was harsh, that his son shouldn't spend time in jail for 'twenty minutes of action.' And worse, the judge ended up sentencing the rapist to only six months in jail, of which he served only three."

"But the public rose up and recalled that judge over it, didn't they?"

"That didn't unrape the girl or result in real justice for the rapist. Sure, his career as a potential Olympic swimmer is over, and he has to register as a sex offender for life, but it wasn't enough. Not as long as that same judge would have given the six-year sentence and thrown the book at some black man the same age without a rich father."

He kept his arms around her. "You'll get no argument from me on that."

"Let's just enjoy seeing our world go by, safe inside our cozy boat."

"With our fireplace and a dog."

"Well, no fireplace. But we can heat things up later." She nuzzled closer to him.

He saw a windmill in the distance, and its blades were turning, but he had yet to see a longhorn steer.

"Hardy?"

"Yeah?"

"Would you teach me some of that self-defense stuff?"

He could have mentioned that it wouldn't have helped that girl who had passed out by the dumpster. Instead he said, "A lot of people think *mano a mano* means man-to-man fighting. It doesn't. It means hand-to-hand fighting. So sure, you can do it. Over eighty percent of those taking my classes back there at the gym were women. They had the same worries and concerns you do."

"Is it hard work and complex?"

"I usually call on a few basic moves that use a person's own strength and momentum against them. It's about cheating in a way, using practiced moves of torque, leverage, and surprise to get an advantage. But I have to use more if I'm scrapping with the same person more than once. Fortunately, that doesn't happen much when traveling along on a highway. It does help, I might add, to have a three-hundred-pound giant of a former offensive lineman as a benefactor willing to step in and toss people about like autumn leaves in the wind."

"People help you because they sense you are a good person and that what you are standing up for is worth the risk to you."

"Of course I'll teach you what I can. We can start right now if you like."

"I like, and you know how you often fret about me doing all the spending—with my father's money, by the way—well, this is the asset you have to give, empowerment to me."

"I'm glad to do it. I can't demonstrate much with this injured wing, but I can talk you through some moves that should help protect you."

"That's what I'm after."

He felt a rush of happiness. He had always enjoyed teaching. It *was* something he had to give, to contribute, and he would feel better if she was better prepared for a world where there were people far too willing to take advantage of or do harm to others.

"I'm only going to try and teach you two things for now," he said. "One is what to do when someone is coming toward you. The other is for when they grab you from behind. We'll practice and practice those. The rest we can work on later."

"I like that."

"What?"

"That you think there'll be a later."

Hardy started with being grabbed from behind. While he went through a couple of responses, he added enough information about pressure points and tender spots to attack for her to use someone's strength and momentum against them.

He found her to be an enthusiastic and quick learner. If his arm had been up to actual hand-to-hand combat, she probably would have been throwing him around the boat's cabin like a rag doll.

In the time they had, he moved on to someone coming at her, first with a right hand and then with a left hand. She improvised well. Once she'd practiced a few go-to moves and grasped the idea that once someone put a hand on her, they were more vulnerable than they thought, she began using all of her slim athletic body to respond with instinct, and the brief muscle training she could hone later.

When they paused for a moment, with her breathing heavy but eyes eager and willing to keep at it, she asked, "Aren't you just a little worried that I might use some of this on you someday?"

"If I try to abuse you or hurt you in any way, then I would deserve whatever you could dish out."

She started to say something and stopped. Instead she hugged him. "Now, show me some more."

"I can't teach you everything in one day," he said, "and you'll have to practice and keep at it. But I can impart one or two things so that, with the element of surprise, you can escape or do some harm to someone bigger than you."

"That's what I want because almost everyone *is* bigger than me."

They kept at it until she had a light patina of sweat and the truck started rolling once more.

She was smiling to herself. Hardy recalled how exhilarated and empowered he had felt when Otto first began to teach him. Even then, knowing only a little and with years of practice ahead of him, he'd begun to picture the next instance of being bullied and what he would do. Some of that glow and growing self-confidence showed in her face now too.

When they sat down to look out the portholes, he felt that she had thoroughly memorized the few moves he'd shared and was far more able to surprise an attacker and take better defensive care of herself than she had been a short while before.

Every now and then, he saw her shifting her shoulders as she sat, going through the moves over and over in her head. He suspected the next person who tried to harm her was in for a rude and deserved awakening. That made him smile too.

Chapter 24

One lingering bit of whimsical memory of the sort they liked to spot about Texas was a mom-and-pop truck stop restaurant sign they'd seen that had said:

No Lone Star Beer

No Amex

No checks

No foo foo drinks

No fries or shoo fly pies

No yuppies or puppies

No wine before its time

No talking to imaginary people

HARDY AND IVY'S TRUCK passed under a yellow-and-red "Land of Enchantment" sign that welcomed them to New Mexico. Much of the land was still as flat as it had been in Texas.

But shadows of mountains along the distant horizons began to hint of places of mystery and wonder, like a far-off Camelot.

Something different began happening to the landscape with every mile they went farther into the state. Hills in the distance grew gradually nearer, and the color of the rocks and soil showed splashes of red, yellow, and orange.

"It's like this land is a dusty bud at first, but even as we go deeper in, it is blossoming into the prettiest, most beautiful state we've seen so far," Ivy said. "We saw green, green, green everywhere so far, on hills and pastures. Here, even the rocks are part of a red, brown, and tan painting I'm glad I got to see."

They stayed glued to the portholes, moving back and forth across the cabin as the scenes developed and changed, in a honeymoon sort of mood, and with Frosty following along to plop down beside them each time they settled.

Hardy had a flash of realization that he was really enjoying this, not just the view but the being together on a road trip, sharing the experiences. He didn't know how it had all happened, but here he was. From trying to avoid Ivy not that long ago, he had let down his barriers and diminished his fears about them being two different sorts of people. He had heard the frog analogy, where a frog in heating water that only gradually gets warmer doesn't realize that he's in boiling water until it is too late. But he felt no alarm, even when he took in the clear picture in his head of what he was doing, what was happening. He relaxed and put his arm around Ivy's shoulder and drew her closer.

More hills and distant mesas jutted up from flat places, while the land along the highway was getting hillier. The contrast of distant colorful rock walls and stands of trees grew gradually into nearer flat-topped mesas with rocky sides of even brighter horizontal stripes of orange, yellow, brown, and red.

"I don't want to miss a single inch of this state." Ivy squeezed Hardy's hand.

"Missing a fair chunk of Oklahoma wasn't my fault," he said. "Okay, it was a little."

When they saw a sign for Tucumcari ahead, Hardy said, "I know that area from it being mentioned in those spaghetti westerns featuring Clint Eastwood and that squinty-eyed Lee Van Cleef. The land doesn't look much different from what it probably was like then."

"Except for the usual fast-food franchises, gas stations, and motels," she said.

"But the land still has a stark beauty. That was the active contrast in those Westerns, a setting worth seeing while danger and possible death lurked all around."

"There's so much more we could be doing," she said. "Maybe someday."

"If we could leisurely explore, there are big stretches of caverns, sand dunes, fields of chili peppers, Native American culture, artist communities, alien landing sites, mountains, deserts, and really, really good Mexican-food restaurants."

"The subject of food creeps onto the canvas of your painting."

"There's only one thing missing in this state," he said.

"Ah," she said. "A coastline. They say people choose between loving mountains or the ocean, and I know where your hopes and aspirations lie."

Their driver kept his usual lumbering pace on the highway. Dusk was settling over the land as they approached Albuquerque.

Hardy could begin to make out parts of the city's skyline. Lights were starting to come on as a growing sparkle of color.

"Oh, Hardy. Come here and look at this."

He followed her over to the starboard porthole. They bent close to peer out.

The Sandia Mountains had been growing higher and nearer to them with each mile. A line of brown grass ran along the highway, with a line of bright green beyond that. The lower parts of the mountains were dark, rumpled, and forbidding, like a sleeping giant. But the setting sun had painted higher patches on the mountaintops a bright flaming orange. Where the royal-blue sky wasn't turning a darker blue above the hills, the clouds were lit as long gold and orange white-edged streaks of brilliant neon color that complemented more than contrasted with the shades and hues of the land below.

"That is as beautiful to see as the northern lights," Ivy said.

The truck pulled off the highway down a ramp that took them directly to a large complex of buildings and a vast parking lot. The driver pulled up to the diesel pumps and filled up before finding a place to park among the other trucks. Then he turned off the engine.

"Oh, good. We're going to be here for the night," Ivy said.

They waited until the driver was out of sight on his way toward the restaurant before they got Frosty down to the ground for his walk.

Hardy watched Ivy struggle a little as she carried the dog. "I can help do that," he said.

"Your arm is lot better. I could tell when I changed the bandages. But don't overdo it just yet. You need at least a day or two more before you put any stress on it."

"If you say so, Doc." He took the leash from her, and together they strolled over to the edge of the parking lot, where the grass grew in clumps here and there in the dusty light-brown soil.

The sky was growing dark by the time they got Frosty back inside to give him food and water.

"Let's just take twenty minutes for me to review those self-defense moves you taught me, okay?"

He nodded and watched as she showed the right responses to every move he made toward her. He knew she was being careful of hurting his injured arm, but she gave the other one a pretty good tug a few times. "You haven't forgotten a thing," he said.

She grinned. "Now I'm off to rustle us up some grub."

"Is that cowboy talk? I thought you were a pirate."

"I have my days when I can be either or both." She winked and went out the hatch.

Hardy went over and locked it.

Barely forty minutes later, he heard Ivy tap lightly on the hatch. He went up to let her in. An intoxicating smell came from the bags she was carrying.

"I found a Latino family cooking away in the back corner of the convenience store. So instead of packaged sandwiches, I got us each an order of warm chili rellenos. They're lightly breaded roasted stuffed poblano peppers, freshly baked in the authentic Mexican way instead of Tex-Mex style. That's a trait of this state. I got them with a Hatch green chile pico de gallo sauce and guacamole."

"You seem to know a lot about food for someone who is prone to eat cottage cheese if left to her own devices."

"I need to keep up my strength, and since we're only eating one meal a day, I think I have room to explore tastes, and that *is* one aspect of travel we should savor."

"Oh, and you got us each a pickled jalapeño with our meal," he said when he opened the lid of his meal.

"I got me two with mine," she said. "But you can have my extra one if your need is great."

"Well, you *are* a spicy little thing."

"I thought we had established that."

"We have. I don't know why I hadn't noticed that before."

"You were too busy avoiding me."

"For obvious reasons."

"Feudal-era ones, if you ask me." She shook her head. "I keep telling you that you pull your weight around here in many ways."

"In a few minutes, I'm going to ask you to take your clothes off."

"Hardy! Don't talk that way in front of our son." She put her hands over the dog's ears then gave Frosty's head a rub.

While she was putting the litter from their dinner into a plastic bag, Hardy switched into his gym clothes and put what he'd been wearing for too many days into a bag. He added the towels they had dirtied washing Frosty and tending to his injured arm.

"Give me your clothes too. And I hate to ask, but I'm down to four dollars. I figure we should get by with one load, but it could run two fifty a load each for the washer and dryer."

She took off her clothes and handed everything to him, including his spare shirt she'd been using as a nightgown. Then she took her time about getting a blanket and wrapping herself in it.

"You're still here?" she asked, giving him a wicked smirk. "The sooner you're done…"

"I hear you, and sorry about needing to borrow money, especially after you bought dinner."

"Hey, don't worry about it. I've got a guy doing my laundry out of the deal, and I'll have clean clothes once again. Sweet," she said. "Plus you can plug in my cell phone and let it charge while you wait on the laundry. I bought a charger cord when I got dinner."

The laundry room was next to the showers, so on the strength of their driver buying fuel, he grabbed a quick shower and shave while all their clothes were washing.

He got back into his gym clothes to sit by the dryer on a folding chair while almost everything they had in the way of attire went around and around. In the shower, he'd felt a jolt when he thought of what might happen if someone made off with their clothes. But none of the truckers came near the laundry room, and only a couple came to use the adjacent showers.

Then, as he was folding their things, he quickly tucked her panties between his jeans and a shirt, realizing he was blushing even as he did it. Her cell phone had charged the while. He slipped it into the small stack of clothes without looking at it. The towels came out cleaner than he could have hoped. He folded them exactly as they had been so they could be stowed back into their cabinet in the yacht.

He looked around as he crossed the parking lot then quickly scrambled up the back, unlocked the hatch, and let himself in. The inside of the cabin was lit only by what light from the parking lot's mercury vapor lights could come in through the portholes. He eased across the cabin, taking slow and careful steps.

She was stretched out on the bed, naked. The blanket was on the floor, and Frosty was curled up on it.

Hardy put the clothes on the breakfast table and went over to her.

"The standard procedure is to wake me by nibbling on my ear," she said without opening her eyes, "or kiss the princess to awaken her from her enchanted sleep."

"We *are* in the land of enchantment." He slid into bed beside her and kissed her.

HARDY WOKE TO LIGHT streaming in through the portholes. It was full daylight outside, and the truck wasn't moving. That was different. He heard the driver climb up onto the yacht's deck and check the hatch and look around. Everything would be shipshape, and there was nothing for him to see. Hardy had even kept an eye on the fastenings keeping the Zodiac secure as well as made sure the life buoy rings were all still in place and hadn't blown away.

He eased out of bed and heard Ivy getting dressed behind him as he went over to a porthole.

"Oh my goodness, it feels good to be in clean clothes," she said.

When he saw the driver go out of sight among the parked trucks, Hardy got dressed himself, and they quickly got Frosty out for a walk. As soon as he was back up and inside the boat, they each headed toward the buildings.

"Don't be long," he said. "The guy might be getting breakfast to go."

"I'm betting he's a sit-down sort of guy who likes his eggs, bacon, and hash browns. Or he could even be a biscuit-and-gravy fellow since we're in the Southwest."

"Just hurry."

Hardy was already in the yacht's cabin when Ivy got back to it. She held up a bag and waved it. "Breakfast tacos, and I got little containers of their peppy salsa." She locked the hatch and brought her spoils to the table. "Also, I got you coffee." She swept a Styrofoam cup out of the sack and put it in front of him. "And I got tea for me."

They were still eating when they heard the driver check the hatch once more.

"See," Hardy said, "he's itching for the open road once more."

"He's probably itching for something or someone or about something."

The truck started up, and soon they were up the ramp and rolling.

They bolted down the rest of their meal and cleaned up. Then they rushed to the starboard porthole to watch the countryside go by.

"The scenery is getting better the farther we get into New Mexico," she said.

He couldn't disagree. Once they were past the city of Albuquerque, the land opened up into fields that ran to lumbering rows of low mountains. The sun turned all the land into bright splashes of color. The ground and sides of hills were red, umber, ochre, and every one of nature's brighter colors.

The hills grew closer until they were right beside the highway in places.

Ahead, two mounds of heaped rocks like ancient pillars worn down, perhaps former mesas, guarded the road on each side. Going between them felt like they were sailing between the Pillars of Hercules.

Even when the land they passed through wasn't high hills and colorful rocks, the scrub bushes and plants that dotted the dusty soil were pleasing to look at and ponder.

"I keep thinking about what it was like on horseback back in the day."

"Just keep your pistol in its holster and don't go starting any gunfights." She chuckled. "Don't get all revved up just because you've had your morning coffee for a change."

"I've had hunches stronger than that coffee."

"You like it stronger?"

"What I'd like is to be surfing the inside curl of a caffeine tsunami. But thanks all the same. Any coffee was a welcome treat."

She slid closer as they looked out the porthole.

They saw something worth seeing all through the day, always with hills or mountains sometimes near and other times farther away.

Frosty stretched out like a puddle of fur to sleep beside them. "I know how he feels," Ivy said, "I've been feeling more lazy or languorous myself."

"It's the elevation. You're feeling the altitude. These Rocky Mountains around us climb all the way up to Colorado. Right now, we're higher up than Denver, and it's the Mile High City."

"I hope you aren't getting any wild-eyed ideas about joining the Mile High Club."

He slid closer and put an arm around her, a little surprised himself that he didn't feel frisky so much as wanting to savor the moment. "I just want to stay glued to the porthole and not miss a bit of this state."

As the truck neared Gallup, they saw lots of signs of where Native Americans had lived and still lived. The Navajo Reservation was closest to them. Though the Zuni Pueblo was out of sight, they knew it and where the Hopi had lived were near.

Souvenir shops were advertised before nearly every exit ramp.

Hardy watched the signs for the reservations go by with a wistful pang—not for the shops, but he would've enjoyed seeing the authentic homes. *Maybe someday!* Come to that, he wouldn't mind peeking into a shop or two to see the pottery, baskets, blankets, and the jewelry, especially if the money went to the tribal craft people who had made them. He bet Ivy would look good with something in silver and turquoise against her skin. But that would have to wait... on a lot of things.

All too soon, they saw signs that they were approaching the Arizona border.

Chapter 25

"I guess we're all growing up a little every day until we stop."

The truck had gotten off to a later-than-usual start. Hardy figured that driving west in the afternoons was the most difficult for the driver, with the sun glaring right in his face, but he was still surprised when the truck started down an exit ramp much sooner than he expected.

"This is way early for a stop," Ivy said.

Then Hardy saw the signs for the Petrified Forest National Park. The truck seemed to be headed right for it.

"This is different," Ivy said. "We're going to a park? This driver hasn't failed once to surprise me."

"He's back in his mode, which in his case is probably pie à la mode." Hardy pointed at a woman behind the glass in the small dark-brown wooden park-entrance station.

The woman behind the window gave a shout. She came out from inside and rushed toward the truck as the driver got out of his cab to meet her with a big hug.

Ivy's head pressed against Hardy's as they both crowded close to the porthole to see their driver in action.

When the woman stepped away from the driver, she went back to the booth and put up a sign instructing visitors that the booth was temporarily closed and that they should put their entrance donations in the box provided.

The driver got back into the truck and followed her as she walked past where her trailer was parked off to one side. She went to a block of several parking spots in a row less than fifty yards from her trailer and picked up a row of orange cones she had used to reserve the space.

The driver, who had apparently managed the maneuver before, turned the truck around so it would be pointing out, and then he parked it.

He got out of the cab with his overnight bag, and he and the woman headed back toward her trailer.

"I've heard that people can stay at national parks for free if they render a service, like manning an entrance booth or cleaning the restrooms," Ivy said. "I just wonder where he met her, unless she's also a waitress somewhere."

"He works in mysterious ways his wonders to perform," Hardy said. "But look at us. We're in a park. How cool is that?"

Ivy led the way up onto the deck and looked cautiously about. "The park doesn't seem overly crowded at all."

Hardy could see only a few people, and some of those were accompanied by dogs on leashes. "Good. It's dog friendly too."

"Let's see if we can fit in." Hardy locked the hatch and went over and started down the back of the truck. He reached up to help Ivy with Frosty. "My arm's getting better every day."

"Just don't try picking up any of these rocks lying about." She pointed toward the nearest chest-high slice of tree trunk on its side that was a burst of brilliant colors mottled black, red, bright yellow, and orange. Its rings were visible, and its outer sides, where there had once been bark, were a seasoned patina of orange-red.

As they walked along a trail, they saw other hikers. They *did* fit right in. Their clothes were clean and their faces bright and fresh, just like the other excited wanderers pointing out whole broken trees on their sides, all with different splashes of color.

"These trees aren't just scared, they're petrified."

"Now, Hardy, you promised."

"Okay. I just couldn't resist that one, lame as it was."

One group of volunteers was gathering up tumbleweeds and putting them in a pile to be hauled away.

"I always thought tumbleweeds were attractive, tumbling along with the wind as they do. But here, they seem to be a pest."

"I suppose anything can be a pest if it's not wanted," Hardy said.

The fossilized old trees glittered in the sun. They paused at a glass-enclosed map of the park. The trails had names that matched and enhanced the tumble of colored rock: Rainbow Forest, Agate House, Crystal Forest, and the Blue Mesa Trail promised a view of the Painted Desert.

"It's not a huge park, but we'll be hard pressed to see it all in the light that's left."

"Yes, and I read that map wrong and thought it said painted *dessert*, and that made me hungry."

"But we have no food." Hardy could see a family at a picnic table, eating.

"There are a couple of breakfast bars and some of your cowboy-belt jerky left. That and water will be fine."

So they headed back to the yacht for a lunch of sorts.

While he was putting food and water into bowls for Frosty, Ivy picked up her cell phone he'd left for her on the table.

"Hey, I got a text from my father."

"Did he wonder when he didn't hear from you for a spell?"

"I told him I was in a no-cell-phone-reception area, Switzerland."

Hardy put the empty dog food can in a bag and started to straighten up, giving her time to catch up on her link with the world.

"Change of plans," she said. "My dad wants me to come to California and meet him when the boat gets there."

"You're way ahead of him on that one."

"But I'm going to have to figure something out. I know—I'll have to get a cab and say I came in from the airport."

"Is it a normal thing for young girls to deceive their parents that way?"

"Normal? It's almost obligatory. You'd understand better if you'd had parents."

Hardy made a long slow turn to her, feeling a sudden wave of tension rippling up through him. "When did I tell you I don't have parents, that I've never known my parents?"

"Oh." Her blush started as a pink that turned to a brighter red that climbed up from her neck all the way to her pale-blond hair. "I... I saw a folder on Dad's desk with your name on it. I guess I peeked inside."

"Why would your father run a background check on me?"

"He does that for every employee. He wouldn't want someone apt to pilfer his stash of champagne, would he?"

"I hope our driver doesn't get the blame for that."

"That's an easy thing to fix."

"What other nifty little things did you find in that background check?"

"Well, for one, you were beaten up at least a couple of times so severely that you were hospitalized."

He didn't say anything. He put the leash on Frosty and led him up the stairs toward the deck.

Before he was out the hatch, she said, "What about lunch?"

"Later."

"Do you want me to come along too?"

"No. I want a few moments alone to think about one or two things."

She stood on the yacht's deck and looked down at him with the saddest eyes as he struggled to get Frosty to the ground without injuring his hurt arm.

"Do you want my help?"

"No."

Once on the ground, he took off at a good pace. Frosty looked back toward Ivy a couple of times, but Hardy didn't.

He didn't know where he was going. He just walked. Inside he felt as wobbly and uncertain as a butterfly born on a windy day.

She lied to her parents and had kept something from him, a fairly big something.

Ivy had halfway chided him about parents and his chivalry just a few days ago. She must have known about his background even then. Had she been testing him?

Expectations are the single place where we most often go wrong about each other.

He walked for quite a while before he realized he wasn't looking at a single thing around him or enjoying it. The place was a wonderland, but for the moment, that meant nothing.

Hardy sat down on a low stump that showed bursts of agate colors on its almost flat surface. Frosty came close and put his head on Hardy's knee.

Hardy took several long, deep breaths and looked around him. He looked down into Frosty's brown eyes, which were fixed on his.

The light shifted as the sun came out from behind a cloud, and the rays from the intensified sun lit up the petrified perch on which he sat and seemed to send out an aura of red, yellow, and orange lights around Frosty's head. The dog's eyes stayed fixed on him, looking up at him with what felt like compassion and understanding.

His hand on Frosty's neck reached out to stroke the smooth, glowing rock. "Will you look at that?"

His head lifted to look around. But there was no one there to look where he was pointing. Frosty looked at Hardy's finger, not where he was pointing, then the eyes swung back to Hardy's face.

"You know, old boy. You're right," he said. "I believe it was one of my regular persecutors—Whit or, more likely, J.J.—who said in that sophomoric lilt of theirs that life is just a meaningless existential hell. Well, they were wrong, so wrong. I dispute them. As long as there are wonders and joys to savor, they were so very wrong."

There were big events in lives that mattered, a death of someone close, an accident, a fire, a storm. But what was roiling around inside him was nothing, a tiny bump, a hiccup.

"And look at you. Are you thinking about being chained and abandoned back at that burned-out trailer? No. You're in the now, the right now, enjoying traipsing across America and having an adventure."

People went by, some in family groups. A couple went past a few feet away, holding hands and looking off at all the frozen-in-time glittering fallen forest.

Hardy shook his head. "I suppose all girls lie to their parents. That's so normal it's almost expected."

Frosty didn't nod, but Hardy felt he seemed to agree. "And what girl could resist peeking into a folder to find out something about someone they kind of have a crush on?"

He dug his fingers deep into the nape of Frosty's neck fur. The dog wiggled his back end, and his tail wagged.

"What am I, eleven years old?" Abruptly, Hardy stood. "Sorry to go all Dr. Phil on you for a moment, Frosty. Come on."

Chapter 26

Hardy walked fast, and Frosty kept up. They made very good time getting back to the yacht even though Hardy wasn't sure which trail he was on a time or two.

Ivy still stood up on the deck, looking down at them, watching them approach. Even from the ground, Hardy could see that her eyes were red.

He waved an arm for her to come down.

She didn't hesitate and scrambled along the ladder and back of the truck as quickly as she could go. Ivy rushed up to him then stopped and waited. "Well?"

"It wasn't fun without you," he said.

She rushed into his arms and held him tightly, and he squeezed back.

After a moment, she leaned her head back and looked into his eyes. She was still crying. "We were doing so well. Please let me back into that bony head of yours."

"The walk helped me sort things out, get things into perspective."

"You should take more walks."

"Can we shoot straight with each other, going forward?"

"Yes. Oh yes, we can."

He took her hand and handed her the leash for her other hand. "Let's do some more of that walking that helps. I'd like to look around and enjoy this time."

They didn't speak for a while, but everything did seem brighter and even more radiantly colorful than before.

They paused to look over a view where the ground dipped down and slowly rose up again. Large, colorful trees had been frozen in place by time and now were scattered across the ground like giant fallen soldiers. In places, shiny facets caught the light and shone brightly and in as many colors as a stained glass window.

The petrified lumber wasn't the only color begging for attention. The hills in the distance were striated with horizontal lines of dark and light shades of brown, grey, and black. Two hills formed cones pointing straight up while other joined rows of hills grew into flat mesas.

"Do you know what my dad told me once?" she asked.

"What's that?"

"Just be sure your love is as fierce as your anger."

"He always seemed a wise old bird."

"You call someone named Reginald a bird, and you'll get to test that theory." She gave his hand a squeeze.

Hardy knew things weren't instantly fixed, but they were better. They were good, and that was a whole lot more than some people could say. They had weathered the tension, for now, and could work on the rest to get back to trust.

The sky was fading but must have felt left behind in the battle for splashes of color because it turned into blurred lines of fading yellow and blue to orange, red, and even lines of burgundy piercing up along the far horizon.

The inside of the yacht was dark as they went down into the cabin.

"We forgot to eat," Hardy said.

"We didn't forget. But we can catch up now. But we're low on water. Maybe I should open some champagne."

"Maybe you should."

At first, she was a little demure, but she slowly worked back to being her perky self. Her kisses, though, were intense, passionate, and more meaningful than ever.

Maybe Hardy was reading a lot into it, not bittersweetness but something else, something richer. Perhaps, he thought, this is how people feel after a storm, one where they've lost a thing or two but are alive and more appreciative than before.

THE TRUCK WAS MOVING when he woke. He was glad they had both visited the restrooms in the night, where there were showers. He had even filled up a couple of the empty water bottles for Frosty and had walked the dog one more time under the stars and part of a moon.

Ivy was humming a tune as they passed the sign announcing Winslow, AZ.

"I was standing on a corner in Winslow, Arizona," he said out loud.

"Funny how that works. When we saw those tumbleweeds, I was thinking about that song where they're 'tumbling, tumbling along.' Now I'm going to have that Eagles tune about Winslow stuck in my head."

"Do you want me to rattle your coconut for you to make it go away?"

"Coconut Head," she said. "That was going to be my stripper name."

When they saw signs announcing "Meteor Crater," Hardy said, "Now, there's something I wouldn't mind seeing. I understand the hole from its impact was massive."

"It's probably too far off-road to see unless our driver knows another woman there. But according to a sign I just saw, we will go right through a town called Two Guns."

"I suppose if there's such a thing as a one-horse town, there can be one with two guns." Such was their mood that morning that she didn't even prod him in the ribs for being corny.

The hills that climbed up gradually into points all around them seemed reddish, sandy, stark, and mostly bare except for yucca plants and large stones dotting them—attractive hiking spots for anyone who liked snakes and other such critters.

To the north of Flagstaff, they caught glimpses of the Kaibob National Forest. Their view was mostly flat open fields leading off to pine trees with a backdrop of mountains.

The afternoon sun blazed at its worst from the west. Shortly after the truck had crossed the state line into California, the driver took an exit ramp down to a truck stop that promised some views of the Mojave National Preserve.

Along the frontage road, Hardy saw lots of cholla cactus plants as well as stark-looking Joshua trees poking up in the distance.

"I'm told that the Joshua tree symbolizes the strength and beauty that can rise from dysfunction," he said.

"Then that's the tree for us." She chuckled as she said it and squeezed his good arm.

"I'm glad this seems to be a full-scale truck stop with food and a chance to restock our water supply."

"And we're not that far from San Diego now. It would be a longer day than he usually goes, but if he busts his hump, we could be there tomorrow."

"Have you ever known our driver to bust a hump?" As he said it, he watched the driver, wearing a khaki shirt this time, saunter off toward the biggest restaurant in the complex.

Chapter 27

"People with bigger biceps are prone to pull things," Otto once said. "Those with bigger triceps push away. You can almost always use some of that strength and tendency to your advantage."

"What if their muscle is in their tongues?"

"You can feel free to bop those in the nose."

THEY GAVE THE DRIVER a few minutes to get into the restaurant, and for all they knew, into his pickup patter with yet another waitress. Hardy said, "We missed Las Vegas. A sign I saw said it was a hundred miles north of us."

"Does everything that happens there stay there?" Ivy asked.

"Maybe a good chunk of your money stays there," Hardy said. "I heard one guy say, 'They cleaned me out in Vegas then hosed the spot where I'd stood.'"

"That's probably how I'd end up too," Ivy said. "But there are a couple of live shows there I wouldn't mind seeing."

"Better keep Frosty in the cabin until I check."

"Check what?"

"The surface temperature. The Mojave Desert is famous for having the hottest air temperature and surface temperature recorded on earth. The mercury can rise to one hundred twenty degrees here. Up in the Death Valley part of the Mojave, they recorded the hottest temperature in America, at one hundred thirty-four degrees. It's also the lowest elevation in North America."

Ivy went up to the yacht's deck with him. They both looked around. It would be a shame to be spotted after coming as far as they had. The air felt warm but dry, with no humidity at all.

She watched as he climbed down to the parking lot and bent to put his hand on the asphalt. "Nope. I could just about cook on this. It's still way too warm. He would blister his paws."

He climbed back up. The sun was beating down on the deck.

"If we spread a blanket out, we can lie on it and watch the sky. It looks like we're going to get one heck of a sunset," Ivy said.

"First, we can see a bit of the desert while it's still light. We'll walk Frosty later. But we'd better leave him in the cabin. We now know he's able to jump to the ground to rescue us, and he's just over his limp from the last time he pulled that trick."

"I fear our fur child has developed a separation anxiety. Do you think we spoil him?"

"At least half of us do," Hardy said.

"Do you think he remembers when he was chained outside a burned-out trailer and left to die?"

"I don't think so. I've heard that dogs live in the 'now.' I suppose that's one of the best possible lessons we can learn from them."

For a while, they walked about the truck stop, a quite large one. They explored, found a row of food trucks along one side, and finally arrived outside the restaurant's window, where they could look inside and see their driver tucked away in a corner table with a waitress bent close as they chatted.

"Surprise, surprise—he's found someone to chat with." Ivy shook her head.

"I don't know. She seems to be enjoying the conversation as much as he is."

"Do you think all these ladies along the way know about each other?"

"I wouldn't be terribly surprised if they do. Look, most professional truck drivers probably can make it across America in half the time our driver takes. But he pokes and dallies and somehow savors places like this." Hardy waved a hand at the truck stop around them.

"Do you think the way he goes about his life is fair to those women?"

"I can't say. I'm not privy to who they are and how they think. All I've seen in his brief visits is that they are as glad to see him as he is to see them."

"You're not judgmental of him, are you?"

"There's no reason for me to project my values, moral compass, or any of that on him. If he was hurting or taking advantage of these women, I might think differently. But from all I can see, the joy of living is reciprocated."

"Would you enjoy multiple partners?"

"Of course not. I can barely keep up with *you*."

"That is the exactly correct answer." She squeezed his arm. "Now, let's go get a quick peek at a desert. I've never seen one up close before."

They walked back to the farthest extreme of the parking lot, where they could look out at the plants, cacti, and a full array of igneous, sedimentary, and metamorphic multicolored rocks scattered across the stark, stony earth. He could see samples of everything from limestone to quartz and granite.

The low, scruffy plants that dotted the sandy soil provided occasional splashes of purple and patches of yellow dots. Behind the open stretches, ridges of hills or low mountains climbed up into the sky in the distance.

"It's as bleak as a moonscape in places," Ivy said, "but with an eerie charm all the same."

Hardy saw something move and pointed toward it. A road runner came strutting into view. It stopped every now and again to look around. When it moved, its tail was pointed down. The tail snapped up to a jaunty angle when it stopped.

Suddenly, its head darted down as it grabbed something that wriggled in its beak when it lifted its head again.

"Did it get a lizard?" Ivy asked.

"Or a snake. I've always heard that seeing a road runner is a sign of good luck."

"If they eat snakes, I'll go along with that."

"Yep. That looks like a baby rattler in its beak."

"If there are snakes around us..."

Hardy bent down and put his hand flat on the asphalt. "We should go get Frosty and walk him. The ground's cool enough for that now."

Frosty was glad to see them when they got back to the boat and even more delighted when they slipped on his leash and took him down to ground level for a walk.

He stood and sniffed the air then took off toward the edge of the desert where they had stood. Once there he stood at point, fixed on something out in that scrub.

Then Hardy saw a ground squirrel scamper across from under the shadow of one low bush and dart for the next place it could hide, but it didn't make it. A kit fox with big ears pounced from behind a low bush and got it, shook it in its mouth, and briskly carried it away. Frosty surged at his leash, but Hardy kept a firm grip on it.

The kit fox looked a sleek little thing, not too much bigger than some Chihuahua breeds. But it easily carried away the limp squirrel in its mouth although it was almost a third its own size.

Ivy looked away. "Let's hope that it's a mom who is feeding puppies tucked away somewhere."

Then a coyote began to howl in the distance.

"It's getting dark," she said. "Why don't I round up some food while you take Junior home."

AS SHE CAME DOWN THE stairs into the cabin, Hardy caught a smell he hadn't had a whiff of in some time.

"I got us Chinese food from a food truck." She put the bag she carried onto the table and began to pull out boxes. "Spring rolls, and for the entrée, I got ginger squid with shiitake mushrooms. Also, chopsticks for each of us, as well as hot tea."

They ate as if they hadn't eaten all day, which was the case.

While he was cleaning up after putting the empty food boxes back into a bag, Ivy wandered to the westernmost porthole, where a glow of light was starting to show through.

"Oh, Hardy. You'd better come take a look. The Mojave Desert sunset is every bit as breathtaking as advertised."

He grabbed a blanket and put Frosty on his leash. Ivy was already started up the stairs, and he followed. They bent over and kept low so none of the other truckers would spot them.

Cloud cover formed the canvas for ripples and sprays of light, shafts of bright orange, golden yellow, pink, red, and here and there, fading bits of blue showing through.

They sat on the blanket and watched every shift and nuance of color, a show that lasted nearly an hour.

After the slow fireworks of the sun setting was over, the sky darkened enough for them to lie back on the blanket and look up at the stars.

"I can't believe this could be our last night of the trip." Hardy's arm was around Ivy's shoulders.

"Have you thought much about what comes next?" she asked.

"Not as much as I should have. I've been like Frosty, kind of flowing with the 'now' of the moments."

"What *are* you going to do once our journey is over?"

"I'm not real sure. Maybe get a job on some ship."

"You do have recent sailing experience, having crossed the continent."

"What about you?"

"I was thinking about looking into the marine biology programs on this coast."

"You wouldn't go back and finish at Yale?"

"For what I'm studying, the Scripps Institution of Oceanography near UC San Diego is one of the best in America or the world. It's also in the La Jolla area, where we have our west coast house."

Hardy could think of several things he might ask about that. He had always thought it the girl's place to bring up awkward relationship questions, like whether or not she would still want him around once she was back around her family. But as Graham Greene once said, "When we are not sure, we're alive." So he said nothing even though he felt a restless niggle in the back of his head. The sky was as dark as it could get by the time they went down into the cabin and were getting ready to climb into bed.

She handed him his flashlight. "Will you read to me?"

"Which book?"

"Dana is fine. Maybe start where he's heading home at last."

Chapter 28

As the sun had faded in their last glance outside, two hummingbirds swirling around and around each other came up to the porthole and seemed to pause, looking in at Hardy and Ivy's faces or perhaps only seeing their own reflections in the glass. In midair, they click-clicked *their long beaks, whirled around another time, and were off into the air in iridescent streaks.*

BEFORE DAWN, HARDY crept out and went down to the ground. He headed over to the restaurant and peeked in from outside. The driver wasn't inside eating his breakfast. He wanted to jog back, but to take it easy on his healing arm, he settled for a brisk walk until he eased up to the truck's cab, put his ear against the outside of the sleeping compartment, and could make out steady snoring.

He waved up to Ivy for her to climb down. She held Frosty down so Hardy could set him onto the asphalt. Frosty shook himself and stretched, ready for a walk.

When Ivy was down beside him she whispered in his ear, "Where's the driver?"

"Asleep in his cab."

"He is so unpredictable."

"I get the feeling he lives exactly the way he wants to live, spontaneity and all."

"Serendipity is more like it."

"He and Huck Finn would have been friends."

"I suppose he *does* waft his way across the highway at his own pace," she said, "much like Huck floating down the Mississippi."

After they got Frosty back up in the boat, Hardy was able to go to the facilities and quickly shave and shower. He was walking back toward the truck, carrying his shaving kit, when he saw the driver walking directly toward him.

His first thought was to dash to one side and get out of sight. Then it occurred to him that the driver had never seen him before.

So he let his heart climb back down from where it was in his throat and kept walking.

"Howdy." The driver gave him a short greeting wave and kept his eyes fixed on the restaurant.

Back at the yacht, Hardy found that Ivy had picked up breakfast tacos and, for him, a cup of coffee that once more had the apparently ubiquitous burned-oil taste of an urn that could use a thorough and complete cleaning.

Her hair was still damp, so she had managed to grab a shower too.

Hardy started cleaning and straightening the cabin, expecting that they would arrive in San Diego shortly and everything would need to be pristine. Ivy tried to pitch in and help, but she didn't have the heart for it, or the experience, so she mostly got in the way. But Hardy didn't complain. He was glad to be doing something together.

Ivy kept peeping out the porthole nearest the restaurant. She finally said, "Ah."

The parking lot was well lighted by the sun when they spotted their driver sauntering their way from the restaurant.

"He's sure in no hurry," Ivy said.

They stayed back from the portholes as they listened to the driver's steps on the deck as he checked the hatch door and looked around topside a bit. Then his shoes clicked as he clambered back down the back ladder.

As soon as they heard the door to the truck's cab slam shut, they slipped quietly back up onto the deck to see what they could of the landscape around them, where the sky was full of the red, orange, and yellow of the day still beginning.

Hardy held Frosty's leash and stayed near the hatch while Ivy eased all the way back toward the stern.

At last, the engine started. Hardy had turned to lead Frosty inside when the dog growled and Hardy heard steps scrambling up the ladder. The head of a tall, lean young man popped up over the stern as he climbed aboard. He had Day Glo bright chartreuse hair hanging in dreadlocks to his shoulders and wore a red T-shirt over jeans. The collar was frayed, and holes had worn through the shirt in several places. In his right hand, he carried a six-pack of long-neck beers.

"I know what you're up to, you stowaways, and I'm coming along too." With his left hand he held a pocket knife with a four-inch blade that locked into place.

"I don't think so," Ivy said.

Frosty's growl grew, and Hardy turned to shove the dog back inside the hatch before he started barking and gave them away.

By the time Hardy looked back, the unwelcome visitor had lowered into a crouch and took off running toward Ivy, knife hand extended.

The truck was rolling toward the parking lot's exit.

Just before he got to Ivy, she stepped to one side, like a bullfighter dodging a toro's horns, grabbed the back of the guy's jeans and T-shirt with both hands and kept him moving, steering him toward the nearest gunwale.

Unable to stop himself, he soared over the side. He landed in a rolling clatter of breaking beer bottles and was slow to rise. He stood slowly to wave a fist at the departing boat, his shirt soaked and the six-pack lying in shattered ruins around him.

"At least he's okay," Ivy said, dusting her hands off against each other.

"Maybe not perfect, but he's now a wiser young man."

Hardy looked into Ivy's eyes, and she turned to him. They glittered with the thrill of her victory. But she waved a dismissive hand and started for the hatch.

"What have I done?" Hardy said. "I just hope you use your powers for good."

"We'll see." She chuckled. "I just used his momentum against him, the way you taught." She looked back toward him.

"I noticed you sidestepped to his beer-carrying side, avoiding his knife, which shows you can also learn from the mistakes of others as well."

Her grin was shy yet showed confidence at the same time.

The truck rolled up the ramp and joined the westward flow on the highway as they climbed back down inside the cabin, where Frosty wanted to sniff and check them over, making sure they were okay.

The adrenalin soon died down, and they got back to the task of tidying up the cabin's insides. All caught up on their chores, they moved to the starboard porthole and watched the flat lands and distant jutting hills of the Mojave go by.

They had gone only a few miles when Ivy shouted, "Oh my gosh. Look!"

Two desert bighorn sheep were bounding down the steep pitch of a slope. At the edge of the highway, they didn't even hesitate but dashed across the westbound lanes right in front of their truck.

Hardy jumped to his feet and raced up the stairs to get up onto the yacht's deck. He was just in time to see the animals start across the opposing lanes and dash right between five speeding cars followed by two semi-rig trucks. As soon as the vehicles had gone past, he could see the sheep jumping and loping with a toss of the big horns on their heads as they cleared the eastbound lanes and started up the slope on that side.

"Whew! They made it!" he called down to Ivy.

At the highway signs for Barstow, the truck exited the highway. Hardy had looked at the map on the wall back at the last truck stop and expected the truck to change highways and get onto I-15 to head south toward San Diego. But that didn't seem to be what the driver had in mind.

"I doubt we went even a hundred miles." Ivy raised her eyebrows when she looked at Hardy. "Can we be up for one more booty-call stop by our driver here?"

The truck went down the streets of the town until it came to a factory outlet mall. The driver turned onto a side street and then onto an even smaller street that ran along the back side of the mall.

He pulled to the curb and parked across the street from what looked like a three-bedroom split-level ranch house with a swing set in the front yard.

"Ah, the kids are away, so Mom will play. Gosh, I hope all these are single women."

"I suspect they are," Hardy said. "We have yet to see any indication at the stops we've made that there's a man in the woman's life. I still think he's just bringing a little comfort into their lives, and they're returning the favor."

"That's mighty generous of you."

"Why don't you see what you can find on your cell phone?"

Ivy got it out and tapped and swept away at the screen for a few minutes. "Oh," she said. "According to what I can find on the internet for this address, the resident is a single mother of two. Hmmm."

"So maybe he doesn't mess around with married women."

"We can only confirm that may be the case this time," she said. "Why is it so important for you to prove our driver is a good guy?"

"I try to give everyone the benefit of the doubt."

"That only proves one thing."

"What's that?"

"That *you* are one of the good guys."

The woman stood on the front porch, waiting for their driver, who gave her a big hug before they went inside.

"He could have easily driven here last night," Ivy said.

"Maybe he was waiting until the kids were away at school," Hardy said. "Or resting until he had the energy and stamina for one more friends-with-benefits visit."

"You're probably right," she said. "But look where we are. There's a mall right across from us." Some cars were parked in the spaces on the back side of the buildings.

"Do you feel the need to shop?"

"Well, I'm supposed to meet Dad when the boat gets to its marina. Since he thinks I was away in Europe, it might help if I had a suitcase and a few clothes."

"Should you get a beret so it looks like you've been to Paris?"

She gave his shoulder a shove. "You can come with, if you like, or you can stay and walk our dog."

"It's me and the dog then. Go shop until you drop. But just remember, we don't know how long our driver is going to take here."

Hardy took Frosty for a really long walk, one he was needing himself as well. He watched the house first, to make sure the driver didn't suddenly come out of it, then he carried Frosty up to the yacht and let him go down the stairs into the cabin. He locked the hatch and then sat waiting beside the porthole that would let him see Ivy come back from the mall.

Time seemed to slip into slow motion and drag. He thought about getting out one of the books and reading. But he was too restless for that, and the more time that went by, the more fretful he was that the driver would come out of the house.

Then he looked across the street, and there was the driver standing on the porch with the woman he was visiting. They were talking.

He looked the other direction but didn't see Ivy. For a second or two, he envisioned Ivy getting left behind and having to grab a cab to take her all the way to San Diego.

He looked the other way. The driver and woman started to walk down the porch stairs then stopped for a moment.

At last, he caught a glimpse of Ivy coming toward the truck. She carried a small suitcase and a bag.

Hardy scurried down the ladder and back of the truck. As he got to the ground to help her, he saw the driver and woman still standing close together, talking. "Hurry!"

He took the bag from her, and she went upward as fast as she could, with him right behind her.

They hurried through the hatch, and Hardy was closing it as he heard the driver climbing up to do his routine check of the deck.

Hardy locked the hatch and didn't move. Ivy was holding Frosty's muzzle to stifle his low growl.

A face popped up and pressed close to look into the porthole. Hardy grabbed Ivy and pulled her and Frosty even closer to get them out of sight while pulling back himself until he couldn't be seen.

The steps went back across the deck, and the driver started back down to the ground.

"It was the woman," Hardy whispered into Ivy's delicate ear.

"Do you think she saw us?"

Hardy shook his head. He opened the hatch so they could hear. Ivy pressed close to him so she could listen too.

"What were you looking for, honey pie?" the driver said. "Seein' if I had anyone stowed down there?"

"You don't even have a key, do you?"

"Nope. Not to this one. Even if I did, I wouldn't bring anyone along but you."

"I'll bet you tell them all that."

"Well, yep. I do."

The woman laughed. "Give all those other women you see my best."

"Will do, honey pie."

The driver must have kissed her then. He climbed up into his cab and started the engine.

"Oh my gosh," Ivy whispered in Hardy's ear. "You might be right after all. He's open with all of them."

"Maybe they're okay with it."

"All we can say for sure is that this one sure seems to be."

"Remember? He was polite to you and not pushy," Hardy said. "Maybe he just goes around, giving some women brief bouts of happiness that they're okay with, and that they need him, like he's some sort of Johnny Appleseed spreading the start of orchards."

"He's sprinkling *something* about across the map. And, yes, he seemed kind and easygoing, if not my type. But still, I would sooner get a lap dance from a hippo than shake hands with that man."

"Am I your type?"

"Yes, you are my type."

"You know you don't have to shake his hand. Just keep hoping he continues to drive as safely and carefully as possible while he gets us the rest of the way. Don't forget, he stopped to free Frosty from that chain when he would have almost certainly died back there."

"But he turned him loose."

"Maybe he's not allowed to have pets that could distract him while he's driving."

"Well, at least we managed to save ol' Frosty here." She gave the dog's head a rub that made him close his eyes.

The truck lurched forward from its parking spot, and the driver took them through town until the truck climbed up a ramp onto I-15 heading south.

"And we're off," Ivy said.

Hardy was looking at the price tag on the Polo Ralph Lauren suitcase she had purchased.

"There was a heck of a sale on that item," she said.

"Yeah, it's marked down to more than I get paid for cleaning this boat from stem to stern."

"The few clothes I bought are packed inside already. Hey, I got you something."

She reached inside the bag and brought out two cardboard cups. She glanced at their sides and handed him one. "There was a little local coffee shop as I came out. I got tea for me."

Hardy opened the lid and took a sniff. He couldn't believe it. He took a sip. "Ah me. Real coffee. This is the best cup I've had on the whole trip, maybe ever."

She giggled. "I hoped it would make you happy. I've seen some of the expressions you make while you've drunk some of the other cups we got."

"You did well—very well. Thanks."

"I got us lunches from the same place." She pulled two containers from the sack and popped them open.

Inside each was a center pile of cottage cheese on a bed of lettuce leaves, surrounded by strawberries, blueberries, kiwi slices, raspberries, and pink-centered figs cut in half.

"I guess I can eat your kind of food since you survived my jerky-eating days."

"Let's sit by the porthole and eat there," she said. "We're on the home stretch now. We should be there today."

Hardy had a mouthful of fruit. The flavors were exploding in his mouth. It had been a while since he tasted anything so fresh. Plus, it had to be decidedly far better than when those British sailors had to suck on a lime to prevent scurvy.

She pulled her cell phone out of her back pocket and checked it. "Yep. Dad's expecting me."

"You know, you don't mention your mother much."

Her smile faded and slid from her face for a moment. But she shook her head and sought to regain it, without being entirely successful.

"We said we would be honest going forward," she said.

"Yes, we did."

"My parents are in the process of trying something new. That's what they call splitting up these days. She is keeping the Connecticut house, and Dad is moving his stuff to our La Jolla house."

"It's lucky you had two, so there was something for everyone."

She twisted her mouth. "I suppose. It's been a little tense for a while. I mean, they don't fight and argue or anything. It's more like they lost or misplaced something that made them interested in each other."

She waited for him to say something, but he had nothing. The only couple he'd known as quasi-parents was Fran and Burt Sanderson. They had acted more like reluctant business partners than spouses. The way they had treated the orphanage children in their care was more like cash crop cattle than little developing humans.

"So now you know why he's moving his pet boat to the west coast and why he's eager for me to visit."

"Is he trying to win you over to his side?"

"I'm already sort of there. Mom and I were never what you'd call close. She kind of tolerates me—coexists, really. It's how she became with Dad too. I guess it's just the way she is. You'd think her favorite food would be ice cubes. Dad once told me that there had at first been a charm to dating an ice princess but that it had melted."

"I've only met your father of the two of them, and he's never seemed real gushy with emotions either."

"That might change if you ever see him in one of his dark and controlling moods."

"How so?"

"Because he can be a little over-the-top protective of me, and he has something of a temper."

"Oh."

"Plus, you've been pretty free and easy with his champagne, as well as with his daughter."

Chapter 29

*E*veryone comes from somewhere and from someone, even if those no longer exist. The single biggest regret of Hardy's life was that he didn't have the beginning of a remote idea, even though he had sought one, about the who and where of his origins. It was like he'd been dropped from the sky into that hellish orphanage, which had since been closed down.

"I ALMOST HATE TO SEE the trip come to an end. I feel like I could keep on riding like this forever." Hardy set aside his empty food container. Frosty sniffed at it but didn't find anything of interest.

"Maybe it's not an end," Ivy said. "Maybe it's a beginning."

"Well, I am sure way the heck away from where I used to be. Talk about getting out of a comfort zone."

She moved closer until her thigh was pressed against his.

Hardy felt overwhelmed by a wistfulness, and he wasn't sure why. It gnawed deep inside him. He wondered if, since he'd come all the way west, to the end of his route, that he felt the way he did because there would be no more west to go toward. He could hardly turn around and start back east. He was at a terminus.

"When you're on the road this long, you become part of the road," he said.

The pace of traffic slowed for a stretch. The truck lumbered along at what felt like about forty miles per hour.

"Oh, I hope there's not an accident ahead," Ivy said, "or that they've set up an inspection station."

"Back at the truck stop, there was an article about agricultural inspection stations. I think they had just moved one closer up to Nevada. It looked like we would miss them and not have to deal with that."

"Sometimes, there are ones for immigrants, but I think they're usually nearer the border. I guess the usual things the inspection stations farther north are after are fruits and vegetables coming in and, of course, cocaine and such."

"With a boat, I read that they're worried about quagga mussels," Hardy said, "which choke out other forms of aquatic life."

"What would we have done if they stopped us and wanted to look down inside the cabin?" she asked.

"A lot of the vehicles with California plates, like this one, are usually waved through. They can't deeply inspect everyone. The hull is pristine. I cleaned it myself. So there would be no need for them to pressure spray it. On top of everything, our driver is clearly a US citizen and has a friendly, open smile, just the sort of person they wave on. Also, I think any shipment of drugs would be coming the other direction."

Mountains seemed to rise up on both sides of them, higher and closer to the road with each mile.

"We're going through the Cajon Pass," Ivy said. "It divides the San Gabriel Mountains and the San Bernardino Mountains east of Los Angeles. Also, and this is for your benefit, we are right now on the San Andreas Fault line."

"Well, don't jiggle around too much, or we could get one of those earthquakes, and our side of the highway would be on the part that splits off and goes out into the ocean."

"They're nothing to kid about once you've been through a good one. They'll rattle your back teeth. That's for sure."

"I guess that'll be something I'll experience in time," he said, "if I'm going to be living here now."

As the hills surrounding them started to lower and seemed to move farther back from the road, the views were mostly of crowded highway and buildings getting thicker in spots.

"Maybe we're just slowed down by all the traffic," she said. "That's southern California for you."

"I read somewhere that one out of every eight cars sold in America is sold in California," Hardy said. "I think it must be true and they're all out on the roads today."

"Now that we're past the mountains, this stretch of California doesn't seem as exciting as it must be to go through Napa Valley." She took his hand and started to pull him across the cabin. "I think you're going to miss some of California too." She led him over to the bed.

Her kisses seemed as eager, pensive, passionate, desperate, sad, and happy as he could imagine. They made his head swirl and the rest of him want to leap up and dance ballet or wrestle a tiger. He couldn't decide which. But in a way, it *was* the tiger because her little naked body was ferocious in its need.

They rose and finished packing up their things then went to look out the portholes. Hardy began to catch glimpses of the ocean as the neared the marina.

Ivy glanced at her cell phone. "I just heard from Dad again. He wanted to see the boat when it arrives, so I told him I'd grab a cab and meet him at the boat."

"That works out pretty well for you."

"Don't worry. Once I've taken care of greeting Dad, I'll find a way to get away," she said.

They went back to the porthole to look out as the driver got off Interstate 15 to head west toward Mission Bay. After a while, he had to get off it and plod through the slower stop-and-go traffic.

The contrast between the New England seaside city Hardy had left behind and the Spanish-influenced architecture with its earth-colored tiles and stuccoes was striking. The plants and landscaping styles told him he was surely someplace else. At first glance, this part of the state even seemed more laid-back to him.

"You'll find so much to look at and explore around here," she said. "There's Old Town, the Del Coronado Hotel area, Sea World, the Gaslamp Quarter, and one of the best zoos and botanical gardens in the world. You'll like the harbor areas, of course, but there are beaches, too, and all kind of places to hike."

The truck's pace gave Hardy a chance to see a skyline of tall buildings in one direction and businesses and residential areas in the other as they wove down through the maze of streets until hundreds of ship masts stuck up into the air, some swaying slightly in the sea breeze. They were approaching the marina at last, the yacht's new home.

Hardy felt every kind of anticlimax possible as the driver finally backed the truck up at the marina where the yacht could be unloaded. It had been a long and event-filled trip, but it was over.

He went through the cabin and gathered up every bit of evidence that they'd been there. He put the last three bottles of water in his gym bag and put together a final bag of trash.

They watched, and the moment the driver walked over to the marina office, they scrambled to get Frosty down to the ground. Hardy had his gym bag with everything he had in it, and Ivy had her suitcase and purse.

They scurried across the street. Hardy put the last trash bag in a container on the corner. They were standing in the shade of a tree when the driver came back to his truck. A specialized forklift able to lift the whole boat rumbled out the largest open door of the marina. Two other dock workers walked along beside it.

The truck's driver, the forklift operator, and the dock workers went about unfastening the straps that held the boat in place.

Hardy watched as the forklift slid into place and began to lift the yacht up from the keel and bilge blocks on which it had sat for the trip. The forklift turned and eased to the dock, slowly lowering the boat into the water. The dockhands held lines to the yacht, and they tied it fore and aft to the dock with its bow out.

"Because it has a cold-molded wooden hull using epoxy adhesives, it can be dropped right into the water," Hardy said, realizing while he said it that he sounded a little sententious and affectionate at the same time. "An old-style wooden hull would have to be wetted down first since it would have dried on the trip and could leak."

The boat bobbed gently in the waves. The dock workers released the Zodiac from its fastenings, and a small crane lifted it, turned it over, and lowered it into the water. A dockhand hopped in, and off it went.

"They'll put it in Dad's boathouse for when the yacht is at its mooring," Ivy said.

The dockworkers hooked the yacht's electric system up to an outlet on the dock. Then they raised the masts into place. They pumped diesel fuel into the tank for the generator and ran a hose across to fill the water tanks.

"Now she'll be ready to hit the waves of a whole different ocean," Hardy said.

"You sound just like Dad. He loves that boat enough to ship it across America."

"I sure spent a lot of time on that boat, working on it to keep it clean and then on our little trip."

"It was a *big* trip," Ivy said. She kissed his cheek. "Listen to me. I'll meet you in front of the Marina Village Conference Center at eight p.m. It's easy to find. It's just over that way." She pointed. "Now scoot before Dad gets here."

Hardy led Frosty away on his leash. Frosty tugged to go after Ivy, but Hardy tugged, and the dog went with him, though he turned his head back to look at Ivy a couple of times.

Hardy found a bench in the shade fifty yards or so from the yacht, where he could sit and hold the leash and still see the yacht. Ivy stood in the sun with her suitcase, looking for all the world like someone who had just arrived by taxi from the airport.

A Lincoln Town Car pulled up, and Ivy's father, Reginald Palmer, got out. Then another younger man got out. The father gave Ivy a hug, and then so did the younger man.

Hardy stood up.

While Palmer walked over toward his yacht, the other guy and Ivy seemed to be talking intently. Then the guy put his arm around her shoulders as they walked over to join Ivy's father.

Hardy waited and watched until all three of them came off the yacht and went over to Palmer's car. The younger guy still had his arm around Ivy's shoulder.

"Come on, Frosty."

Hardy stood and led the dog along the row of docked boats until they were out of sight. He felt a lump in his throat that seemed half again as big as the yacht.

"I don't know, Frosty. I just don't know."

Frosty looked up at him. Hardy had the last two cans of dog food in his bag, as well as a bowl for water. But he didn't have a single dime in his pockets.

While he loved being near the boats and the ocean, he was reminded of the time on the other coast when he had roamed, smelling restaurants that were cooking tasty meals while his stomach had growled. He felt more alone than he could ever remember feeling.

He walked Frosty around until he located the Marina Village Conference Center. Then he walked and walked some more until Frosty began to slow down. Instead of his eagerly sniffing brisk pace, he now plodded along, looking up at Hardy from time to time.

"I'm sorry, old fellow. This is probably too much of a good thing for you."

He went back to the center and lowered himself to a set of steps where he could see the front of the building.

A guy in a faded tie-dye shirt and worn jeans carried a guitar case to the far end of the center, where more people went by. He opened the case, took out his guitar, and left the guitar case open at his feet as he played—busking. Any other day, the music would have been relaxing, a treat. But as Hardy watched people toss coins and the occasional bill into the guitar case, he was only reminded of how little money he had on him. Even if he had so much as a kazoo himself, he doubted he could generate a single coin coming his way. Given Hardy's limited musical abilities, he figured his only chance for a tip would be if someone paid him to quit making that racket.

Some of the people in the Great Depression must have felt that way as they shoved hands into pockets and couldn't even feel a dime to rub. The effect was also emotional, leaving him with a hollow ache that made him rub Frosty's back and head even more than usual.

The afternoon passed as slowly as Hardy could ever remember. The sky changed from wisps of clouds in blue to a dimmer hue as colors began to show along the horizon to the west.

Every twenty minutes or half hour he got up, and they went to the corner, where he could see a white-faced clock on the inside wall of a hardware store that was closed for the day.

Finally, eight p.m. came and slowly went by. Then it was nine. Still no Ivy. At nine thirty, he said, "Come on, buddy."

He felt gutted and had no place to stay and no money, so he headed back toward the boat. He put his hand in his pocket and felt the key. It was solid and real, so he had that. There would be power and water now, but no food had been stocked yet. *Ah well.*

Once he was on the dock, he looked in all directions then lifted Frosty and hopped over onto the deck. He unlocked the hatch and locked it behind himself as he went below.

The boat was so familiar, yet it seemed more hollow and empty than ever.

He sat on the cabin's floor for a while, not wanting to muss the made bed. The sound of waves lapping against the hull was soothing, but his insides were aching, like that coyote he had heard howling at the moon back at the desert.

Frosty moved close and rested his head on Hardy's leg. The sky grew dark outside the portholes, the last red of the sunset on the water faded to black. Then the night dragged on while he sat and thought far more than he should have, too restless to sleep and hungry and hollow on top of that.

He reckoned that it had to be somewhere around midnight or one a.m. Then more time dragged by as slowly as it could go.

After what must have been hours later, he heard furtive steps on the deck. They stopped. For a while, he heard nothing. Then he heard them again. The steps went to the hatch and seemed to hesitate, then he heard a tap and another.

Frosty growled low and rose from Hardy's leg to rush to the door, then he stood on the steps and stayed quiet with his tail wagging.

Hardy went closer. He could hear a faint voice, a loud whisper.

"Hardy? Hardy? Are you in there?"

He unlocked the hatch and swung it open. Ivy stood there. Even in the dim light, he could see that her round cheeks were wet. She'd been crying.

She rushed down into his arms and gripped him as tightly as she ever had. "Oh, Hardy. I couldn't get away. Then I couldn't find you. I started looking everywhere. This is the only place left. It seemed so empty, and I was afraid... afraid I'd lost you, that I'd lost you forever."

Hardy heard loud footsteps go past on the walkway along the docks. "Shh. Shh." He tugged her over to where he'd been sitting on the floor. Frosty tried to wriggle between them, but Ivy moved the dog aside, and he had to settle for sprawling across their legs.

"I saw you," Hardy said, "with a guy. He had his arm around you. Then you didn't show up."

"I'm sorry. I'm so sorry." She hiccupped. "That was Edmund."

"Edmund?"

"I know. It couldn't be Ed or Eddie. His name had to be Edmund in that circle. He's someone Dad was trying to encourage me to see more of. He even flew him out here. Edmund's family is old money. But I was breaking up with him even though I'd never really gotten around to going with him. Then I got stuck with having to drive him to the airport. Dad said it was the least I could do after breaking Edmund's preppy-school heart."

"Didn't you get along?"

"We were compatible," she said, "but just not with each other." That made her giggle. She put her arms around Hardy and squeezed tightly. "Just FYI, he was very polite, but he had the personality of a wet sponge."

"And you don't prefer that? Or would you rather have quirky?"

"I like all of your little quirks and characteristics, even unto all the tiny bones in your head."

"When I thought about it," Hardy said, "had too much time to think about it, I wondered if I'd been some sort of casual fling since I'm nothing like your crowd."

"Oh, you knucklehead," she said. "You think you're a giver with nothing to give. But that's not so. You give plenty, more than you know."

"I guess," he said. "What would you like to do?"

"I'd like to hold you awhile, a long little while, if you don't mind."

"I don't mind. I don't mind at all."

Chapter 30

Ivy's eyes looked quite big this close to his face as she grinned and pressed even closer to Hardy. Though it wasn't cold, he kept his arms around her soft shoulders. They sat huddled together on the cabin floor. It seemed to him that hours had gone by. Frosty pressed as close to them as he could get. Occasionally, they talked in low voices, and just as occasionally, they sat through long patches of silence, listening to the gentle slap of waves against the hull. They both petted Frosty.

"You know, this is the most you've ever talked to me, opened up, and let me see the real you," she said.

"That surprises you?"

"It baffles me more than a little. You have a degree in communications, and you gave something like a seven-word valedictorian speech."

"Ironic?"

"Very, and heavy-handed at that. I figured sooner or later you'd have to talk... or just explode from holding everything in."

"Perhaps some of that comes from growing up in an environment where sharing thoughts or opinions was often violently discouraged."

"But there's something else," she said, "something more."

Hardy hesitated then said, "Do you know where you come from?"

"Do you mean Connecticut?"

"No. Your family. Your heritage. From where did your line of people come?"

"I'm told Welsh-Irish on my mother's side and stuffy British from Dad's kin."

"Do you know who your grandparents are?"

"Of course."

"And you especially know who your parents are," Hardy said. "I have none of that, not a scrap, not an idea."

"Is that what's been bothering you?" she asked. "That and thinking you're poor?"

"I don't have *any* money in my pockets right now. That's kind of poor."

"Well, that doesn't matter a red cent to me. I know you're bright, work very hard, and that you're going to make it on your own someday. All I think you need is your chance—and to trust in yourself more. Grades in school won't deliver that, but how you perform in life will."

"Do you really think so, believe so?"

"I knew when you taught me those moves to protect myself that your whole life must have been one battle or confrontation after another in an effort to achieve your way out of what you perceived as a bad situation," she said. "As I learned and practiced, I felt my own confidence growing, and I began to understand you better."

"And you still like me?"

"Like you more."

They had been rattled emotionally there for a short stretch and felt the effect of having been through a small storm, from which they had to heal, assure each other, sometimes with words, sometimes with the comfort of just being close.

Inside his head, Hardy had always felt like some little old man even when he'd been the youngest student in classes. But everything that had happened had made him feel younger, far younger, perhaps even a little more naïve than usual. That wasn't a bad thing. It meant there was a myriad of things to see, experience, and learn, much of it for the first time. He felt fresh, ready, and as alive as he'd ever felt.

Outside the portholes, the night was the deep dark of just before dawn—too late for people heading home from taverns and too early for even the earliest risers who would take their boats out onto the Pacific.

Hardy said, "Shh. Listen." He pointed to the deck above them.

"Footsteps?" Ivy asked. "Who would get on the boat at this hour?"

"Well, I doubt it's the dock crew taking the yacht out to put it in a mooring."

"What, then?" she whispered.

"That's someone taking the boat."

A low growl came from deep in Frosty's throat. He sat up, alert.

"Now what?" Ivy said.

"It sounds like someone's untying the lines to the dock." Hardy slowly got to his feet.

Ivy did, too, and clung to his arm. "Are you afraid?"

"Of what? Dying?" he whispered. "I was when I was little and got picked on a lot. Now, I just aim to enjoy as much of life as possible as it rolls by."

"Hardy!" she whispered.

"I know. The boat is moving. We're being towed."

"Not sailing?"

"No. The sails are still furled."

Whoever was towing them was staying as quiet as possible, pulling the yacht all the way out of the harbor into the Pacific.

The movement of the boat slowed, and the boat began to turn and rock in the waves.

"I think whoever was towing the boat has stopped," Hardy said. "The yacht's on its own now."

"What's that sound?" Ivy asked.

"Now someone is unfurling the main sheet. We're getting ready to sail."

"Where do you think we'll be going?"

"My bet is south," Hardy said. "Just a hunch."

The hatch rattled. Someone was trying to open it and come below.

Frosty growled and shot across the cabin then went up the stairs and started barking loudly.

"Oh, you mean well, old boy, but we didn't need that," Hardy said.

"Yo, Byron! Dere's someone down in there!" a man outside the hatch yelled.

"You better get 'em outta there," someone, probably Byron, yelled.

A fist started to bang against the hatch.

"It's strong enough for that," Hardy whispered to Ivy. "Let's hope that's all they've got."

Ivy pulled Frosty back away from the hatch and put him on his leash. She tried to keep him quiet, but it was too late for that.

Someone was wrenching at the outside of the hatch, tugging, twisting, prying, but getting nowhere.

Hardy looked around. He could think of no place to go or to hide. Nor could he think of any way this would come out well if they just stayed below until the boat got to its destination, wherever that might be.

Then something hard began to bang against the wooden hatch. The banging continued relentlessly. At first, it was just a hammering noise. Then tiny splinters began to pop from the wood on their side. Hardy saw a flicker of steel that pushed out the next bit of wood. It looked like a knife point.

The tip of a knife began to show through with each pounding blow. More and more of the knife was getting through with each hard stab. The blade looked like it might be on a fixed blade sheath knife like a K-bar. Hardy knew that, in time, that would be enough to get someone through the hatch and at them.

He looked around for a weapon of any kind. Now, the Spartan minimalism of the cabin worked against him.

He went over to a cabinet and took out a bottle of the Dom Perignon. When he came back over with it, Ivy said, "Now is hardly the time."

He held it by the neck and shook it in the air. "It's the only thing we have."

"Should I get one too?"

"I doubt you'd be very handy at swinging it around as a weapon."

He stepped up onto the stairs so he would be between Ivy and whoever was outside, hacking away at the hatch.

The effort seemed to take an hour. At first, a hole began to appear, and it was growing rapidly. The hole in the hatch widened until the hand and knife punched through it. Then the knife wielder chopped to make the hole bigger. At last, he grabbed at it and ripped the hatch open. Hardy braced himself and clenched the champagne bottle's neck tighter.

The man on the deck above them was probably in his twenties and wore a dirty white tank-top undershirt, the kind that was once called a wife-beater shirt. His hair was dark and very curly, with long thick sideburns. His eyes had the squinty, watery look of someone who was a heavy drinker. The face showed no sign of human caring or sentiment at all. His was the face of someone who had done far worse things in his life than what he was contemplating doing now, and he would do it with no compunction or regret.

He put the knife away in a sheath at his side, the kind with a sharpening stone in its own separate fastened flap. His other hand held a gun, which he lifted and pointed at Hardy's face. "I think you'd best come up out of there."

Ivy had moved closer to Hardy. Frosty barked and snarled, pulling at his leash, trying to get up the stairs and at the man.

"Tie up that damned dog, or I shoot it," the guy said. But the barrel of his pistol had moved and was pointed toward Ivy. He knew Hardy's weakness.

"Don't worry, Ivy. He doesn't want to shoot and risk knocking a hole in the boat and making it leak."

Hardy could see from the guy's face that he hadn't even thought of that.

"Tie up the dog, or I shoot it," he repeated.

"What are they going to do with us?" Ivy whispered to Hardy.

Hardy didn't have any doubts. The ocean was a big place, and people pushed into it this far out from land were never found. There were far too many hungry critters waiting below.

At the first chance, he and Ivy, probably Frosty too, would be over the side and headed for Davy Jones's locker.

Ivy led Frosty over to the breakfast nook table and tied the end of his long leash to it.

Hardy was thinking hard for a scrap of anything he could possibly do, but he had nothing. Maybe he would have a chance for something once he was up on the deck. He glanced back at Ivy, then he went the rest of the way up the stairs.

Dawn was just lightening the sky to the east, enough so that they could see reasonably clearly as Hardy and Ivy went up through the broken hatch. One man was at the helm, another broader-shouldered muscled one stood on the deck near the bow, and then there was the man with the gun still way too close to Hardy to miss.

The man at the helm was a tall swarthy man with his oily brown hair pulled back into a ponytail, a few days of dark growth on his chin, and small golden rings through his earlobes. His hair was receding at the front so it looked like his head was pushing itself out into a sunburned brow. He seemed to know what he was doing, had probably had a lot of experience sailing or perhaps just at stealing sailing boats. He was making the most of the wind and cutting cleanly through the waves. He grinned at them in a way that was anything but friendly. His was a pirate's kind of sneer, the kind Hardy might expect from someone up to stealing a boat.

They probably looked small and insignificant to the helmsman, the tiny skinny girl and Hardy, who was no kind of giant. They seemed to be a joke to him, one at which he would laugh out loud soon, right after three loud splashes.

Chapter 31

Once he and Ivy were up on the deck, the man with the gun reached and grabbed the bottle out of Hardy's hand. He shook it in the air. "Hey, look what I got, Rueben."

He tossed the bottle to Rueben, the stocky guy with short blue hair who was standing in the bow. He caught it. When he glanced at the label, he yelled, "Whoot!"

He shook the bottle in the air and held it close while he yanked off the foil and started untwisting the wire.

These guys know damn all little about champagne, Hardy thought, *but that could be a good thing.*

The cork burst out of the end of the bottle, shot across the desk, and slammed into the low cabin wall with a bang like a gun being fired. Champagne gushed in a fountain of foam from the end of the bottle.

The instant the man with the gun turned his head to gape for a second at all the foam, Hardy kicked. He caught the bottom of the gun hand with his toe, and the gun flew up out of the hand and landed with a plop into the water going by.

The man's eyes opened wide. One hand shot down toward the knife handle while he lowered his head and charged at Hardy.

"Someone else's anger can be your friend," he'd told many of his students in the self-defense courses he taught. A person isn't thinking clearly or reacting in a thoughtful or trained way when smoke is coming out of his ears.

Hardy slipped his left arm inside the right arm of the charging man as he came to him. His palm went to press down on the shoulder in a come-along hold. He put his other hand on the back of his own hand and pressed even harder down, forcing the guy to bend forward at the waist while still trying to swing his left fist across the front of his body toward Hardy's face.

They spun around a few times while the guy twisted and struggled to get away from Hardy's grip or at least punch him.

Hardy used the guy's charging momentum to keep him moving forward. Before the guy realized it, they had come to the edge of the deck.

Hardy let go of his hold and gave the guy's back an abrupt, hard shove. The guy kept going, with his arms waving around and around like he was trying to catch air as he tried to stop. He didn't, couldn't. Instead, he shot over the gunwale into the water that was surging past the moving yacht.

"Well, crap!" the helmsman yelled.

Hardy had figured out he must be Byron. Hardy never got the name of the guy he had just thrown overboard.

Byron started to turn the boat to go back for the guy. The sails crackled as they luffed before catching a bit of wind so Byron could tack back to where they'd been.

Rueben dropped the sopping champagne bottle to the deck and tried to rush Hardy. He was a big fellow, broad where Byron was tall, but he moved unsteadily since Byron was having to steer the boat through rougher waves going back the other way, which made them bounce like a bucking bronco horse.

Hardy could see the guy now who'd gone overboard. Byron was steering the yacht closer, and the guy was swimming toward it.

Rueben wore boots instead of deck shoes, and he was having a hard time navigating the rolling pitch and yaw of the moving deck. He slipped and fell almost onto his face on the wet teak.

The champagne bottle went around and around like a game of spin the bottle. As it neared Ivy's ankles, she bent and grabbed it by the neck and flipped it overboard, where Rueben couldn't use it as a weapon against them.

A wave pitched the boat again, and Rueben slithered across the deck toward her and grabbed Ivy's ankle.

She gave a high-pitched desperate scream, with her eyes open wide. She twisted and turned as she tried to tug free of his grasp.

Rueben scrambled to his knees and pulled her to him, probably thinking that Hardy, who was across the deck from them, would have to go to her aid.

When he'd had her by the ankle, Ivy hadn't known what to do. But as soon as he had his hands on her, she had trained for that. Hardy could tell she had absorbed, memorized, and practiced his words of instruction when she found the pressure points inside Rueben's thumb and forefinger along with the nerve by the little finger, squeezed as hard as she could on those, and twisted his wrist.

The second his other hand let go of her, she grabbed the wrist she held with her other hand and twisted and rolled, standing up straight again with all the pressure of her little body lifting him up onto his toes before flopping him to the deck on his back. Hardy felt a surge of pride. She had been a good and eager student, able to apply what she had learned.

Frosty came bounding up the stairs onto the deck, trailing his leash rope behind him. He had worked his way loose from where Ivy had tied him.

He rushed to Ivy, getting between her and the fallen man, snapping at Rueben's hands and snarling so fiercely Hardy could barely recognize the dog. He was all wolf now and protective of Ivy.

Rueben struggled to his feet as fast as he could. He tried to reach across the snarling dog to grab Ivy's blond hair. She hadn't practiced for that contingency.

Frosty lunged first to one side and then the other, trying to keep him away from Ivy. Rueben kicked at the dog with his boots while still reaching across and trying to grab Ivy's hair.

Hardy rushed across the deck to push Frosty aside to keep him from getting kicked and to place himself between Rueben and Ivy. The moment Hardy's back was to Rueben, he grabbed Hardy from behind with both arms around him. Rueben probably couldn't believe his luck. He had him, at least.

As soon as Rueben put his big arms around him, Hardy immediately dropped into a squat. His weight bent Rueben at the waist. When Rueben's head came forward with his torso, Hardy's arms shot up to grip him tightly around the neck, then he abruptly stood back up while he pushed back hard with his hips and butt, sending Rueben flying through the air over the side of the boat and into the water.

Hardy grabbed one of the lifesaver rings off the top of the cabin and tossed it in Rueben's direction. "You're probably going to have to share!" he yelled.

Byron let go of the ship's wheel, pulled a blackjack the size of a marlin spike out of his back pocket, and smashed at the yacht's radio. Then he charged around the helm toward Hardy. From the first time Hardy had seen Byron's "fox in the henhouse" sneer of a smile, he had figured him for the sort of fellow whose first preference in a fight would be to get in a sucker punch. Hardy didn't intend to let him have the chance for that.

Left with no firm hand at the wheel, the ship's sails snapped and crackled, and the boat twisted in the water, tilting hard to one side to begin rocking in the waves.

Ivy grabbed the edge of the cabin and clung tightly.

Byron avoided going right at Hardy, lifting his bludgeon high he went toward Ivy, probably planning to get her out of the way first. He didn't look like he had any intention of putting up with her or Hardy's jiu jitsu nonsense.

He was almost to her when Hardy saw a furry black blur shoot across the deck and slam into the side of Byron. Both the tall man and the dog shot over the side into the water.

The rest of Frosty's leash was trailing rapidly across the deck toward where he'd gone.

Hardy rushed across the deck and slammed his foot down on the rope, stopping it. Then he bent and grabbed it to start pulling as hard as he could. The yacht had slowed as it turned to its side to rock in the waves, and Frosty was dog-paddling as hard as he could.

The second he was close enough to the hull, Hardy bent, shoved his arms elbow deep into the water, and grabbed the dog, lifting him onto the deck. Wet and shaking, Frosty still managed to wag his tail and rush to Ivy, who clung to his neck.

"Throw that other lifesaver buoy out to that guy! They pop right off," Hardy yelled to Ivy as he scrambled to the helm and grabbed the wheel to steady the rocking boat and get it on course to go back toward the harbor and marina.

Byron was swimming as hard as he could toward the boat. He grabbed at its side to try to pull himself back aboard.

But Frosty rushed to him, barking, snarling, and snapping at his hands until he let go.

Ivy tossed the life buoy ring in, nearly hitting Byron in the head with it.

The yacht's sails caught the wind and pulled away from Byron in a rush, going much faster so that there was no way Byron could swim to catch up, though he seemed to be trying.

Ivy held Frosty's leash, and the two of them came to stand beside Hardy. He had the boat under control and had started his tacking maneuvers that would allow him to get them back to where they wanted to be.

He glanced back and could see just a bit of color from where the three men were bobbing about in the waves and swells.

"It was nice of you to give them something to hang onto," Ivy said.

"Like I've said, I'm not out to kill anyone. I just want to protect you and Frosty here."

"Frosty kind of did his bit protecting us as well," she said. "I'm sure glad you were able to get him back onto the boat."

"That's supreme sacrifice for you, him going overboard in the process of saving us. Getting him back aboard was the least I could do."

"Oh, you're hurt too," she gasped.

He looked at his left arm. Blood was seeping through the white bandage where Ivy had been so careful to keep his wound dressed.

"Probably happened when that blue-haired goon, Rueben, grabbed me. There's nothing I can do about it now until I get us to shore."

"I'd help you steer the yacht if I knew what to do," Ivy said.

"And I'd let you so I could clean up the boat as much as possible. This little diversion has left things a mess."

"All fixable stuff." She looked around the deck and fixed on the ruined hatch. "We're alive. That's the important thing."

Chapter 32

"*Victory can have a bitter as well as sweet side,*" *Otto had once told him.* "*You throw a guy across a room into a jukebox, and you'd expect applause. But no. Somewhere, karma is rolling up its sleeves and is about to let you have it.*"

IVY HELD FROSTY'S LEASH and stood close beside Hardy at the helm. She kept a nervous eye on his arm, where the blood was still red and wet where it had seeped out through the formerly white bandage on his arm. But even the throb in that arm didn't keep Hardy from savoring and enjoying the feel of the ship's wheel and the sight of the vast sea around them.

"You did a heck of a job back there," Hardy said.

She grinned. "It was your lessons. They really came in handy. I know what you meant about muscle memory. I didn't have to think much. I just knew what to do when I felt that guy's energy just where I knew I could use it against him."

"Well, you were a very good student."

The pleasing tang of the salty air pushed and rubbed against the skin of his face like a nibbling, tickling living thing. He took in a deep breath that felt almost affectionate, like coming home.

The sets of waves and swells layered one on another, a line of silver on the crests of the waves, for as far as he could see. A lone gull swooped close enough to have a look at their sailing craft then swept off and was soon out of sight.

"I wish he hadn't smashed the yacht's ship-to-shore radio," Ivy said, "or that my cell phone wasn't back at Dad's place, getting charged."

A whirring drone in the sky was coming their direction. It became a steady chopping that grew to a roar as a helicopter buzzed along the horizon then moved closer, circled around them once, beating up the water beneath it into a froth. Then it took off again.

"It won't be long now," Hardy said.

"Long for what?" she asked.

"You'll see."

Twenty minutes later, they saw a speck ahead on the water. The speck grew into a white boat with a red diagonal slash.

"Is that a...?"

"Coast Guard cutter," Hardy said. "Yep, and they're coming right at us."

The cutter slowed as it came closer. Everyone on its deck seemed to be staring their way.

Hardy couldn't stop without letting the yacht flounder around. The cutter eased even closer and dropped a red RIB into the water. Men swarmed into it, and it headed their way. As it came alongside the yacht, several of the Coast Guardsmen swarmed aboard. They had even brought a dog crate big enough for Frosty.

Each of the men wore sunglasses as well as a blue uniform with a bright-orange Search and Rescue (SAR) vest, the kind Hardy had learned cost over five hundred dollars each, his tax dollars at work. One wore a Coast Guard ball cap, while the others all had their heads bare with their hair buzz cut short.

They wore sidearms, pistols in holsters low on the hip the way gunslingers once wore them.

Two of the men grabbed Hardy and threw him down on the deck and put handcuffs on him. He knew not to struggle or resist. Their actions were automatic, their training kicking in.

One sailor took over the helm and furled the sails while the others fastened a towline to the bow of the yacht.

Frosty growled and barked at the men. To protect him from harm, Ivy led him into the crate and closed the door. Then she let herself be handcuffed.

"Did you know I'm the daughter of the man who owns this yacht?" she said as they sat her on the deck next to Hardy.

"We'll straighten all that out as soon as we get to shore, missy."

"Missy?" Ivy let out a hard breath of air.

"Your real boat thieves are floating around back there a ways," Hardy said, looking up at the two guards who stood over them.

One of their guards stepped away. Hardy supposed he was communicating with the cutter.

"I guess our pirate days are over," Ivy whispered to Hardy.

"I'm guessing that wouldn't be a very good thing to kid about with these guys. I have yet to see one of them smile."

The men loaded Hardy, Ivy, and the crate containing Frosty onto their rigid-hulled inflatable boat and took them over to the cutter. The Coast Guardsmen on the cutter's deck all wore the bright SAR vests too. Most of them wore dark sunglasses.

A female petty officer, with her blond hair pulled into a bun at the back of her head, picked up Frosty's crate and carried it as she led Ivy away.

Hardy was led away in the other direction while the men stowed the RIB. The cutter was already moving forward, towing the yacht behind. He looked back and caught enough of how they cranked their RIB up a ramp to stow it. It was probably a good sign, he thought, that he enjoyed seeing how they did that. He was learning, and life for him was always all about learning.

Two Guardsmen with almost no expressions held him by the upper arms and led him down a narrow hallway and into their sick bay. A female Health Services Technician was tugging on latex gloves. "Put him down over there"—she pointed at a gurney fastened to the deck—"and you'd better take off the cuff on that arm so I can patch him up."

They took off the cuff that had been on his left wrist and locked it onto the gurney.

The technician raised an eyebrow at the men but went to work cutting away Hardy's blood-soaked bandage. She had brown hair that swept down, framing her face nicely, and she was capable of a smile every now and then. Nor did she act as serious and gung ho as most of the other Coast Guardsmen he'd met. She seemed almost human, like a civilian.

"We're going through some tough times out here on the high seas," she said as she worked. "Everyone's especially alert and prepared for anything, and they often get just that. These Guardsmen act the way they do because they need to. There have been days with real danger and shooting."

Hardy nodded.

She leaned closer and said in a low voice, "You don't look like much of a pirate to me. I heard about the flag the guys saw below."

"My wooden leg fell overboard, and my parrot flew away."

She chuckled as she tossed the wet, bloody bandages into a tray. She began cleaning and disinfecting the wound.

"I told them about the guys who *did* steal the boat," he said. "They're back there, bobbing around somewhere. And there's the boat that towed us out from the dock in the first place. It must be back around that harbor someplace."

"I'm not the one you need to tell that to." She glanced up at the men who stood with folded arms, waiting for her to give Hardy back to them.

He watched her pull the sides of the wound back together. It hadn't split as deeply as it had been before, so he had been mending before those guys had wanted to play roughhouse.

She finished by wrapping fresh gauze and tape around the spot. "Now don't go swinging around on any ropes for a few days."

The two waiting guardsmen rolled their eyes at that. They handcuffed his wrists together once more and led him out of the sick bay and farther down the hallway and into a small holding cell of a room. They sat him on a steel bench and fastened the handcuffs to it.

"Do you want to hear my side of the story?"

"Not yet," one of them said.

"There'll be plenty of time for that," the other added.

They went out the door and left him there to strictly meditate his thankless muse, as the poet Milton once said in his poem "Lycidas."

Hardy had a lot of time to wonder how Ivy and Frosty were doing. The guardsmen had been a little gentler with her.

He had time to think about those men he had left out there bobbing in the waves too. He hoped they had all ended up with something to hang onto and that they got picked up before they got hypothermia. Or worse, that something swimming below hadn't noticed them with interest.

But he couldn't feel all the way sorry for them. If they had had their way, he, Ivy, and Frosty would have been in the water and without any lifesaver rings, either.

He felt the rumble and power of the big cutter beneath him. It probably wasn't going as fast as it could since they were towing the yacht.

He recalled sitting on a straight-backed chair at the so-called orphanage, waiting for Mr. Sanderson to call him into his office den and punish him for something he hadn't done. But he was going to get a licking all the same.

It seemed that for all his life, he had been alone. For a brief while there on their land-bound boat voyage, he'd been part of something, almost as a tiny family. But now, he was alone again once more, so very alone.

Then he sat for a while and tried to think of nothing, of nothing at all.

Chapter 33

Having sailed both the Atlantic and Pacific Oceans, all he had to do was close his eyes, and he could hear the regular sound of waves climbing the shore, accompanied by the cries of gulls.

HARDY SAT IN THE PASSENGER seat beside the uniformed Coast Guardsman driver of one of those unmarked cars of the Coast Guard Police Department that few people would mistake for just another vehicle on the road.

So far, his driver had looked straight ahead and had only spoken briefly to say, "Normally, I don't do this sort of chauffeuring around. But you must be a friend of somebody who knows somebody."

"I'm not so sure about that."

The driver shrugged, so Hardy spent most of the ride looking around at the city then the countryside around him as they left San Diego and headed into La Jolla. From what he could make out from the driver's shoulder patch, the Coast Guard was part of Homeland Security. This was his first opportunity to examine one of the patches so closely.

They turned up a drive that went up to a private residence on a hill. The drive looped around the front steps of what looked like a pretty stately two-story home, a mansion of sorts. The lawn was well maintained and the grounds landscaped. The house was mostly white with red trim.

As they pulled up and stopped, Reginald Palmer himself came out the front door and started down the front steps toward them.

Hardy stepped out of the car, aware that his chin and cheeks were covered in a growth of stubble and his clothes were a mess.

Palmer gave the car's driver a curt salute, which was returned. Hardy suspected Palmer had some military in his background, navy from the cut of his jib.

He turned and started up the steps. "Follow me."

No hello. No handshake. Hardy watched the stiff, upright back in front of him and wondered what kind of trouble he was in. He followed through a house he would have liked to take a closer look at but had to step briskly to keep up at all.

They went up a marble staircase that bent to its left on its way to the second floor. He followed Palmer down a hallway and into a room where one glass wall looked out across the ocean. Palmer waved toward a red leather seat across from the desk and went around to sit down behind the desk.

Ships in bottles sat in front of bookshelves crowded with leather-bound books. A quite large painting of a clipper ship dominated the other wall. Ships' steering wheels and other nautical-themed gear hung on the wall around the painting.

"I suppose you're wondering what this is all about, what just happened, and what comes next." Reginald Palmer was no kind of easy smiler on his best days, and his face looked as stern as Hardy had ever seen it.

Hardy sat down. "Yes, sir."

"Did they tell you anything at the Coast Guard station?"

"No. They just bunged me in the jail or brig, they might call it."

"But then they let you out?"

"They said I was free to go and gave me a ride here."

"They told you nothing?"

"They asked a lot of questions I couldn't answer."

"Perhaps it would help if I let you in on the bigger picture of what happened."

"It couldn't hurt. Well, maybe it could. But I'd like to know." Hardy's insides were hopping and tossing around like sumo-wrestling butterflies.

"First of all, the Coast Guard was able to pick up those three men who you left floating out there."

Hardy started to say something, but Palmer held up a hand.

"They were just wharf rats, the kind desperate enough for money to do anything. They were supposed to take my boat down to Mexico, alter its identity, and then use it to haul cocaine up into the states. With the land border tighter than ever, the cartels have had to increase their efforts by air and sea to get product into America."

"Why didn't those Coast Guard people tell me any of this?"

Palmer shrugged. "There's more. The smugglers have used small submarines, fishing vessels, and most recently, small high-speed panga boats. They're similar to the cigarette boats used to traffic drugs on both coasts. These are usually painted in soft green colors that camouflage them at sea. They're very fast and have a low profile, which makes them hard for radar to detect."

"How does your yacht fit into that picture?"

"There are hundreds of thousands of boats out there on the ocean, fishing, recreating, sailing, or just puttering about. The Coast Guard thinks the latest trend is to round up as many everyday sorts of boats as possible and use them to haul the product north. If they lose a few, so what? It's a business, and the numbers—and profits—are on their side. And they're using more of the kind of men you made walk the plank in the same way, disposable men who are paid well when they succeed and who are ignored when they fail."

"How about the boat that towed yours away from its dock so those guys could try to sail it off to be used that way?" Hardy asked.

"That's the biggest break of all for the Coast Guard on this one. One of those wharf-rat boat thieves, who claimed, by the way, that you threw him around like a rag doll when you tossed him overboard, sang like the entire Mormon Tabernacle Choir and ratted out the boat owner who did the towing, and he has turned out to have direct ties with one of the cartels."

"Did that guy I supposedly tossed mention having a knife and a gun he might have used on Ivy?"

"No, but Ivy brought it up. She said you were very brave."

"You're probably wondering how I happened to be aboard your boat when it was taken."

"Not really. I was brought up to speed on that by Ivy, who also came clean about not really being on a tour of Europe. She apparently thought a tour of truck stops along our nation's interstate highways held greater thrills."

"There were some moments."

"Travel seems to have had a positive effect on her veracity. She has been straightforward with me about a number of things."

"What kind of trouble am I in?"

Palmer frowned, and his face grew as stern as Hardy had ever seen it. Then, in spite of himself, he started to chuckle.

"You were always a good worker, and I never paid you nearly enough. That boat is a pet of mine, and you took good care of it, defended it, and even rescued it."

"Do you want me to keep cleaning it as long as I happen to be on this coast now?"

"No. I want to talk to you about something else, something that's more challenging. It means you'll have to work a helluva lot harder than cleaning a boat, and you'll have to use that brain of yours too."

Hardy tilted his head. He could think of nothing to say, so he sat and waited.

"You see, I bought a clipper ship a while back. It was always a dream of mine. I want you to work on her as a crew member, to work your way up until you're fit to be the captain and manager of sailing it for whale watching and ocean clean-up groups. Captain McAbrams plans to retire in two years. He wants to groom someone to take his place. I've known him for years. He's a firm but kind captain."

"Hasn't flogged anyone?"

"Well, hardly ever." Palmer grinned. "His salary comes from my businesses. One hundred percent of what the boat makes goes to charities. Cleaning plastic out of the ocean is just one of them."

"Oh."

"Another thing. I wouldn't be your boss. The ship is meant to be self-sustaining. The captain runs the business. I'm strictly hands-off. It's the deal I have with McAbrams, which he kind of favors, by the way. If I wish to be a passenger or use the boat's services, I pay just like everyone else. Will you think about it?"

"I'll do more than that. I accept outright."

"It's no gift, son. You're going to have to work very hard. And you'll have to show a profit... which we can turn over to charities. That's been part of my dream, too, and I want you to be a part of it. If you make a living at it along the way, that's okay too."

"Yes, sir."

"Are you sure about your decision?"

"I am."

"I ask because people, young people like yourself, should never have to rue a decision for years and years. If you change your mind, you let me know."

"Okay."

"You see, I know of a fellow, a driver of trucks for one of my companies, who lost his wife quite suddenly a few years back when she was killed on the highway by a drunk driver. I thought he might grow lonely in his cab going back and forth across America. So I offered him the opportunity to work his way to being manager of one of my shipping terminals, where he could be around people more. But he turned me down. He's still driving for me to this day, and I know few people who are happier. Now, I must tell you, there are box turtles faster than that man, and he soaks up his per diem expenses like a biscuit sopping gravy, but he's careful, safe, and I can't think of anyone I'd rather have driving one of my trucks. He's the one I asked be given the charge of bringing my pet boat all the way out here."

"Really?"

"Oh, I've had his dispatcher confide in me that he's had one or two women call and ask when he'll next be coming through where they live. So we've figured out a bit more about him than he's let on about. But we've never had a complaint. If anyone is a model for being happy, it's that man. I could learn a thing or two from him."

"I see."

"Now, here's the thing. I have relearned one thing a little later than I should have. It's that happiness is as slippery as a greased-up eel. You have to grab it and hang on or at least know when you've lost it and then go and find it again. That boat is one of the few things that makes me truly happy, so I'm glad it's being worked on right now to restore it to its glory. I always appreciated how you treated her and cared for her."

Hardy tilted his head. He mulled over whether Palmer was still talking about a boat.

"Do you understand, and do you stick with your decision?"

Hardy nodded slowly, still soaking it all in. "Would you consider one thing?"

"What?"

"If I ever do get command of your clipper ship, would you consider renaming the boat *Ivy*?"

"Well, we'll see when that time comes." Palmer stood up. He seemed to be holding back another of those rare grins. "You show yourself out. You know the way." He held out a hand, and Hardy shook it.

Hardy went down the stairs slowly, feeling more numb than excited. He took in the paintings on the walls, a tapestry, and some vases on stands that looked old. His mind felt as overwhelmed as being washed overboard, but in a good way. Still, he had a whole lot of questions, many of which were answered the moment he went out the front door.

There sat Ivy behind the wheel of a sky-blue Subaru Crosstrek. "Hop in, sailor, if you're going my way."

His mouth hung open, and he forced himself to close it. He slid into the passenger seat and closed the door.

"Most environmentally sound car I could find," she said.

"Did your dad buy it for you?"

"He *does* spoil me."

"Where are we going?"

"You'll see."

She drove back down toward the marina where the yacht was docked.

"What's going on in the off-ramp that passes for your mind?" she asked.

"Just wondering if we are going to get into the boat again."

"No. It's getting its hatch repaired anyway. Despite fond memories, we're not going there."

She pulled up and parked in front of a row of condominiums that looked out over the docked boats. They were close enough to the ocean to hear the gulls and the sound of waves and to smell the salt in the air.

Ivy led the way to the door of the condo on the end and opened it.

She waved a hand. "Voilà!"

He looked around. The interior was decorated in Spartan fashion, which he liked. The front window looked out to the docks.

"You can see the ocean from the second floor," she said.

She stood waiting.

He shook his head, not knowing what to say.

"It's yours to stay in. Dad owns the condo and used it for business stuff or as a getaway. He wants you to have it rent free for a year until you're established in your new job. You did take it, didn't you?"

"I did." He looked around, knowing his eyes were open wider than usual.

"We discussed whether you could live in the guest house there at the La Jolla home. But we decided that if you want to come after me, we shouldn't make it too easy, that you should have to work for it."

"You're pretty confident, aren't you?"

"Quietly smug, I'd say, or secretly hopeful. Oh, and there's something else."

She led the way into the kitchen.

The appliances were all the brushed silver of steel, and the table and chairs were teak. A white envelope lay on the table.

"That's yours," she said.

He picked it up, opened it, and saw a thick wad of hundreds. He looked up from it at her.

"Part of it is the money Dad owed you from cleaning, which he never got to pay you when you disappeared. Part of it's a reward for rescuing the boat from those thugs, and I didn't even tell him about the other time you saved it. I didn't want to get our driver in trouble. The rest is an advance on your salary so you can get a few things you need to start a new job and set up your home here."

She had used magnets to put up their silly pirate flag on the fridge door. Hardy reached and swung the door open. The only thing inside was a bottle of Dom Perignon.

"That's for later," she said. "You might want to shower and shave. Now that you're loaded, you can at least take me to dinner. Your shaving kit is in the bathroom. I was able to salvage your gym bag from the yacht before the repair crew started to work on it, and I bought a few things for you to wear that are fresh and clean and in your closet. So get cracking. Hup. Hup."

He went up the stairs, still looking around in disbelief.

The bathroom door was open, but the adjoining bedroom door was shut. He reached and opened it.

Frosty came bounding toward him, jumping up onto him, his tail wagging as hard as it could.

"I saved the best for last, don't you think?" Ivy said from downstairs.

Hardy hugged the dog, and his eyes filled with moisture he was glad Ivy couldn't see. He didn't much trust his voice either, but he managed to say, "Yes, you did. Indeed you did."

About the Author

Russ Hall is author of fifteen published fiction books, most in hardback and subsequently published in mass market paperback by Harlequin's Worldwide Mystery imprint and Leisure Books. He has also co-authored numerous non-fiction books, most recently *Do You Matter: How Great Design Will Make People Love Your Company* (Financial Times Press, 2009) with Richard Brunner, former head of design at Apple, *Now You're Thinking* (Financial Times Press, 2011), and *Identity* (Financial Times Press, 2012) with Stedman Graham, Oprah's companion.

His graduate degree is in creative writing. He has been a nonfiction editor for major publishing companies, ranging from HarperCollins (then Harper & Row), Simon & Schuster, to Pearson. He has lived in Columbus, OH, New Haven, CT, Boca Raton, FL, Chapel Hill, NC, and New York City. Moving to the Austin area from New York City in 1983.

He is a long-time member of the Mystery Writers of America, Western Writers of America, and Sisters in Crime. He is a frequent judge for writing organizations.

In 2011, he was awarded the Sage Award, by The Barbara Burnett Smith Mentoring Authors Foundation—a Texas award for the mentoring author who demonstrates an outstanding spirit of service in mentoring, sharing and leading others in the mystery writing community. In 1996, he won the Nancy Pickard Mystery Fiction Award for short fiction.

Read more at www.russhall.com.

About the Publisher

Dear Reader,

We hope you enjoyed this book. Please consider leaving a review on your favorite book site.

Visit https://RedAdeptPublishing.com to see our entire catalogue.

Check out our app for short stories, articles, and interviews. You'll also be notified of future releases and special sales.

9 781948 051996